FOR EVERY HEART, THERE IS A SEASON

For Norman and Ethel Thayer, it might well be the final blossoming of all their years of love together.

For Chelsea, it might be the last chance to capture the love she needed before it was too late.

For Billy, it might be his first lesson in love on the road to growing up.

It was summer—

ON GOLDEN POND

"Sensitive, loving and welcome!"

—*St. Louis Post-Dispatch*

ON GOLDEN POND

A PLAY

BY

ERNEST THOMPSON

with an Introduction by
Richard L. Coe

A SIGNET BOOK

NEW AMERICAN LIBRARY

TIMES MIRROR

Publisher's Note

This play is a work of fiction. Names, characters, places, and incidents are either the product of the author's imagination or are used fictiously, and any resemblance to actual persons, living or dead, events, or locales is entirely coincidental.

Copyright © 1979 by Ernest Thompson
Introduction copyright © 1981 by The New American Library, Inc.,

Film Photos © Copyright 1981 ITC Films, Inc. All rights reserved.

Published by arrangement with Dodd, Mead and Company, Inc.

 SIGNET TRADEMARK REG. U.S. PAT. OFF. AND FOREIGN COUNTRIES REGISTERED TRADEMARK—MARCA REGISTRADA HECHO EN CHICAGO, U.S.A

SIGNET, SIGNET CLASSICS, MENTOR, PLUME, MERIDIAN AND NAL BOOKS are published by The New American Library, Inc., 1633 Broadway, New York, New York 10019

First Signet Printing, December, 1981

9

*For my parents, Esther and Theron Thompson,
who are not Ethel and Norman Thayer but might
be. With love and great admiration.*

RICHARD L. COE has been "Critic Emeritus" of *The Washington Post* since 1979, having joined the paper in 1938. He served on *Stars and Stripes*, Middle East edition, during WWII and became Drama and Film Critic of the *Post* in 1946. He lectures at the Smithsonian Institution and is also Professorial Lecturer at George Washington University.

INTRODUCTION

by Richard L. Coe

Because TV's prime time *West Side Medical* collapsed after its initial thirteen weeks, actor Ernest Thompson's friends assumed he was concentrating on beach sports yards from his Santa Monica digs.

"Not at all," he laughed, quite slyly, pulling his bicycle toward the door. "I have something for you to read while I'm gone." He handed his visitor from the east three plays in tidy, blue-bound folders.

That was how I met *On Golden Pond* the summer of 1978.

I read his plays in order of their creation, finding the three one-acters of *Answers* rich in character-born dialogue and the two acts of *Lessons*, about two college productions of *The Glass Menagerie* a decade apart, theatrically ingenious. Finally, *On Golden Pond* brought the heady assurance that here was a tightly written play of life-loving bite which proved that my young actor-friend indeed was a playwright.

Two summers later I'd be standing by a New Hampshire lake watching such notables as Katharine Hepburn, Henry Fonda, and Jane Fonda embodying those characters who had moved me so much that morning by the Pacific. So precise had been Thompson's stage directions they left little for a stage director to do. The screen play, which he had adapted himself, simply moved some of the action outdoors.

None of those three powerhouse stars ever had acted together, and despite a widely-publicized actors' strike—from which a special dispensation had been laboriously, tactfully, obtained— the atmosphere on the set had that serenity and subliminal tensions which mark *On Golden Pond*'s father-mother-daughter reunion. From director Mark Rydell to the crew's humblest go-fer tingled confidence that these months of filming were exceptional experiences for all.

The reason for this assurance lies in the play itself, richly comical on the surface, universally moving below. At a playwriting period of labored omphalaskepsis (absorption with one's own navel!), it was a cleansing relief to come across the sort of play many theatergoers have been missing, its acceptance and affirmation of life not unlike the qualities Thornton Wilder poured into *Our Town*.

This family reunion for the eightieth birthday of Norman Thayer, Jr.—he insists on that junior—is not really so placid as its New England, midsummer healthiness may suggest. He and Ethel, aged sixty-nine, have arrived at the lakeside cottage where they've spent every summer since their marriage forty-eight years before.

Coming from California to join her parents after a long absence, upon which Ethel rather acidly remarks, Chelsea Thayer Wayne, we'll realize, does not recall her childhood with happiness. Nor has her broken marriage been much joy. She's described as forty-two, "quite pretty, a bit heavy, athletic-looking, tan, a nervous type, something dark about her, but she has her father's humor."

Norman's humor also is dark. In fact, he seems a bit of a crank. His eightieth birthday finds him long but reluctantly retired. He's gruff with the phone operator and when Ethel remarks cheerily on neighbors as "a very nice, middle-aged couple. Just like us," Norman sniffs: "Middle age means the middle, Ethel. The middle of life. People don't live to be 150. . . . You're old and I'm ancient."

Norman also grumbles social prejudices. Learning that Chelsea's latest boyfriend is a dentist, he snorts: "Oh, God. He'll be staring at our teeth all the time. Why does she have such a fascination with Jewish people?" When Ethel replies "Who said this one was Jewish?" Norman answers "He's a dentist, isn't he? Name me one dentist who isn't Jewish." He's not really prejudiced when he learns of the death, at ninety-seven, of Miss Appley who lived most of those years with Miss Tate: "There's something to be said for a deviant lifestyle."

There is a crustiness, yet a recognizable likeability about this angular fellow who's spent most of his life as a teacher. It comes to us that he'd confidently expected Chelsea to be a boy and that he's evidently felt betrayed ever since. He'd brought her up to know all the major league records and she'd tried all her childhood years to dive a perfect backflip. She is aware that she's been a lifelong disappointment to her father. Small words and withheld gestures can be telling.

Trying to keep peace between the two for over four decades, Ethel Thayer has developed wary control, pleased, in a sense, at keeping them apart but also anxious at this stage of their lives to ease from both the respect and love she deems they properly owe one another.

Ethel wants to come to grips with their barriers. With Chelsea has come indirect aid, Chelsea's new companion, Bill, and his twelve-year-old son of a divorced marriage. Billy. After Norman has jolted Bill about sleeping arrangements and Billy accepts schoolmasterly commands to read *Swiss Family Robinson*, it develops that Chelsea wants to leave Billy with her parents while she and his father tour Europe.

Ever so quietly, almost unnoticeably, conflict comes when Chelsea remarks to her mother that "coming back here makes me feel like a little fat girl. . . . You never bailed me out."

Ethel glares: "Here we go again. You had a miserable childhood. Your father was overbea ing, your mother ignored you. What else is new? Don't you think everyone looks back on their childhood with some bitterness or regret about something? . . . Life marches by, Chelsea. I suggest you get on with it."

That's plain parental speaking long out of style.

Before the five scenes are over five lives will have been altered, not with jolts or high theatrics but within what's thought of as old-fashioned family custom, avoidance of issues, a little give, a delicate take, a bit of a push, a gentle shove.

Read the play slowly and you'll find the tensions under Norman's sharp, teasing humors as well as the girlhood links, years apart, between Chelsea and her mother, who had spent her own girlhood in this cottage, built by her own father when she was a child. These are intelligent, middle-class Americans, recognizably individual, caught up in the universal family problems of getting along together.

The critical scenes between mother and daughter and father and daughter remove the pall of sentimentality which trickles through this summation. In the playing there has to be bite and sharpness. Striving for sympathy and charm must be avoided. This is not a story of growing old but a reflection of what it takes to love one another.

Add Bill, Billy, and Charlie, the postman who has been delivering mail around the lake by boat since he and Chelsea were teenagers, and you have the rest of the characters, well-defined roles all.

But the three central parts are special ones, defined within strikingly brief lines, only occasionally more than a couple of sentences. It's always seemed that actors, who know just about how much can be mouthed at a time, ought to be able to write sayable lines, the kind of writing basic to this realistic genre. Thompson's acting career helped his playwriting.

Just about as soon as play agent Earl Graham had given him the script, Craig Anderson, director of one of New York's most respected Off-Broadway houses, the Hudson Guild, contracted to stage it in mid-September, an exceptionally quick birthing. Frances Sternhagen and Tom Aldredge, players passionately admired by their peers if not so familiar to the general public, were assigned to act Ethel and Norman. They played them so winningly that two years later they still were Ethel and Norman.

There would be three New York opening nights within a year. After the Hudson Guild's 30 performances, producers Arthur Cantor and Greer Garson (yes, the actress) determined on a Broadway production, with tuneups in Wilmington and Washington. Sternhagen and Aldredge continued as the stars, with Mark Bendo, Stan Lachow, and Ronn Carroll, as Billy, Bill, and Charlie, and with Barbara Andres replacing Zina Jasper as Chelsea. After that run of 128 performances plus 6 previews at 43rd Street's New Apollo (snatched from sordid flicks and its 42nd Street entrance), the same cast would resume again, under still other producers, at the Century for another 253 performances, stretching the New York run into a two-season stand. Other playwrights that season got a lot more critical attention but none achieved anything like a fraction of the 417 performances for Thompson's play.

There would be two noteworthy audiences on the detour from the Hudson Guild's Twenty-third Street a mile north to the Apollo.

The most personally affecting was in Washington, where Thompson's brother Paul, a Navy legal officer, happened also to be serving as a social aide at the White House. Learning that his aide's brother had written a play to be performed in the Kennedy Center, President Carter turned over his box to the Thompson family for opening night.

For father Theron Thompson, who, says the author, "is not Norman Thayer any more than my mother, Esther, is Ethel Thayer, although they certainly could be," it had to be a deeply satisfying evening. Before the New York run had finished Theron Thompson's long illness would end in his death.

The most professionally affecting of those early viewers arrived alone for a Thursday matinee in Wilmington's Playhouse Theater after a rainy morning drive from New York. She bought a single seat at the box office (no special treatment for her), afterward had upbeat words for the cast, which had heard she was in the house, and then drove back to Manhattan's Turtle Bay.

That solo long-distance driver was Katharine Hepburn.

She'd begun her professional career not far away, in Baltimore, fifty years before, and hers must be one of the most photographed faces in world history. Small wonder everyone knew she was in the house.

Come back to the autumn of 1934. From the second balcony of Washington's National Theater, I saw the premiere of a play from which not much was expected. Its co-author, Marc Connelly, was the most noted name connected with *The Farmer Takes a Wife*, about the start of the Erie Canal. The players were known generally as character actors: June Walker, Margaret Hamilton, Ralph Riggs, and vaudeville's Herb Williams. The least known of the principals was the young hero, played by one Henry Fonda.

As soon as this black-haired, lanky fellow came on, he registered, and if you register instantly in the top balcony you've got something. Looking like a brush-stroke undecided whether to be a question mark or an exclamation point, Fonda would continue to register in just that openly quizzical way for the next forty-six years. Somehow, in 1934, you knew he would.

Leap forward to 1960. Touring the land's media centers under auspices of the Brothers Warner was a blue-eyed, strawberry blonde with a firm jaw, pouty lips, and uppercrust acent. She'd "done" a New York play which had flopped but seemed to prefer talking about her life as an art student in Paris rather than the slight movie she was promoting, *Tall Story*.

Art was then a novel pitch for a movie ingenue. You tried drawing the conversation round to her famous actor-father, but about the most she would say about him, was that "he's a pretty good painter himself." Pressing a point, you remarked that also acting in *Tall Story* is the same Marc Connelly who had given her father his first big stage role and his first movie part. "Maybe Connelly will write a play you could do together?" "That'll be the day," Jane Fonda had replied in those toney tones of mother Frances Brokaw's Little Old New York and of Emma Willard's upstate finishing school.

Twenty years later, according to Thompson, it will be Jane who pulls this three-star package together. "Hepburn wanted to do Ethel but said nothing about who as Norman. Henry wanted to play Norman but said nothing about who as Ethel. It was Jane who worked it all out. She's a very orderly, persuasive lady. She told me she was determined to do a picture with her father and that it was an absolute natural for Hepburn to be Ethel."

Jane's determination to act her father's daughter was formidable. Henry was seventy-five and it had been widely publicized, to encourage others, that he used a heart pacer. Katharine's birthyear was in all the books, 1909. The script set the period of the year precisely, from mid-May to mid-September.

Complicating all was an incipient actors' strike which would come to a head just when the film was to start rolling. An agreement was signed by Jane's company and the allied Marble Arch Productions with the Screen Actors' Guild that terms of any new contract would be honored.

In the course of shooting this would prove an embarrassment to Jane, noted for her liberal stands. At one point, she'd fly to the coast to appear in a benefit for the strikers. Another provision in the agreement was that the set would be closed to press and photographers, not at all endearing to New England media.

Down Easters had expected the filming to be in Maine, for not only does the script so specify but the Thompson family long has had a summer home there. Unit producer Bruce Gilbert, however, had settled on Big Squam Lake, not far from Center Harbor on New Hampshire's Lake Winnipesaukee. Big Squam is free of jerrybuilt shacks; its bungalows and large homes which rim the lake are almost invisible from the water.

As with all top-budget Hollywood-on-the-Road shootings, there's an army of specialists, all housed within a twenty-mile area. There's even the truck and tent labeled "Michaelson Food Services, Inc.," which has rolled all the way from Sun Valley, California, to serve daily specials such as lobster, crab, filet mignon, or trout almondine—three-course, quality lunches.

There is the camera crew of veteran Billy Williams. There is the lighting detail, the sound man and his staff, carpenters needed to improvise level platforms for the shifting cameras. There is the script department to check out each of the hundreds of setups and contribute differently colored pages for rewritten scenes dictated by such exigencies as weather, noise, and the unexpected. There is the wardrobe staff, the property and makeup departments, and the hairdressers. On the sidelines sits a nurse with her satchel for cuts, bruises, and insect bites.

All this is under the artistic control of Director Mark Rydell, a Westernized Bronxite, even-tempered and usually smiling. He laughs:

"Why shouldn't I be smiling? Look at the cast and crew I'm working with, the best, the absolute best. If I blow this one, it'll be my own fault.

"After Jane had lined up her leads, I was chosen to direct. It must have seemed very iffy to Katharine. Soon as she heard that I'd directed *The Rose*, off she scooted to see it. That must have been a shock. From Bette Midler to Hepburn? Then she had *The Reivers* screened and could see why I'd been picked. 'A fine picture, a fine picture,' she told me. 'Had I seen only *The Rose* I would have thought Jane had gone out of her mind to choose you for so quiet, mellow a film as this.' "

Now all is quiet for a scene. Ethel Thayer has sent Norman off to pick berries from the long-familiar patch down the road and he is back with an empty pail. Why? Thayer confesses: "I got lost."

In Fonda's face there is despair, in Hepburn's the realization that this crusty, independent man of hers is crumbling. Two lifetimes are crystalized in an instant.

The scene ends, the cameras stop, and in the hush, some onlookers brush moisture from their eyes. "Whew" murmurs one of the men.

Later, Hepburn confides: "Working with Henry brings tears to my eyes. He is so sensitive, so giving an actor. I've always admired him, of course, but working with him for the first time is a marvel."

And later Henry says forthrightly: "What a joy it is acting with Katharine. She can play all the levels of a scene and always is able to add something so fresh with a slight gesture or look."

Later yet, on the hunch that they wouldn't have said such things to the other, I relay what each has said to the other. Hepburn's superbly mobile face brightens: "Oh, I'm so glad. I didn't know. Thanks for telling me." You know she means it. Fonda's eyes light up: "Golly, did she really say that?"

He stretches his long, blue-jeaned legs from his canvas arm chair and muses:

"Think of how lucky I've been these last few years. At a time of life when there aren't many leading parts for an old duffer like me, I've had four beauts—Clarence Darrow in the one-man *Darrow*, Justice Dan Snow in *First Monday in October*, Colonel Kinkaid in *The Oldest Living Graduate*, which we've just finished doing on stage in Los Angeles, after playing it from the Texas of author Preston Jones on TV, and here's Norman Thayer. Beautiful parts, all of them.

"Didja know I might have done George in Albee's *Who's Afraid of Virginia Woolf*? But the agent never sent it to me. Didn't think I'd like it. I hit the roof and asked Albee to send me, personally, his next one.

"He did. *Seascape*, and I phoned him right after reading it that I'd love to do it. In the same mail was another script, *Darrow*. I read it after phoning Albee. What a situation! I had to call Albee back to renege. Awful thing to do. But I couldn't have missed *Darrow*.

"This amounts to a family party. Shirlee and I have been married for eighteen years, longest of my talked-about marriages. She's my real keeper. Nobody gets to me except through her. I'm the beekeeper, the only one in Bel-Air I expect. I enjoy farming at our place. Must be the most expensive darned farming land in the whole earth. Think of that, me from Nebraska, Bel-Air farmer. Shirlee's mother's looking after our place while we're here and I told her that if anything dies, it'll be her fault.

"Jane and her husband, Tom Hayden, and her children—Vanessa, now twelve, and Troy, eight—are here, and they live in the next largest house.

"Katharine has the big one. She so charmed the people who earlier had taken a two-week, mid-August lease that they just decided to go somewhere else so that she can stay put. Katharine was going to take Shirlee's and my house and we were going to move to Jane's and where Jane was going to go I'm darned if I know. Jane's in charge of all this.

" 'Course, Chelsea's nothing like so large a role as she always plays. Didja realize that Jane's won two Oscars—*Coming Home* and *Klute*—and I've never won one?

"This house here. Our designer Steven Grimes added a story for the staircase we have to have. The house can be restored to how it was when we got it, but the owners may choose to leave it as it is. The Burwells, next door, had no idea that a film company was moving in for the summer. Fifty feet from their house with all this equipment and bustle. I'm sure they couldn't have been pleased.

"Katharine decided that someone had to play diplomat so she did. She went over and introduced herself: 'I'm Katharine Hepburn. We're making a movie next door and I do hope we're not ruining your summer.' Can't you hear Katharine saying that? She told them to come over and watch any time they liked and of course that changed the atmosphere completely. Someone should have done it earlier, but trust Katharine. She thought of it and did it. Great.

"Luck plays such a part in this profession. Suppose I hadn't gotten *Mister Roberts* when I did, just after the war. We started the rehearsals in nineteen forty-seven and I was still playing him in fifty-one.

"See that chap over there?" says the original Mister Roberts, pointing to actor William Lanteau. "I played Roberts in a company with Willy when he was just starting out.

"He's just arrived to play the mailman, which he'd done in the Julie Harris-Charles Durning stage company in Los Angeles. Another actor was signed for it but Rydell proved his mettle as director when he said 'We should have taken the guy who did it in L.A.,' and darned if he didn't replace the other actor. Cost a small fortune, I guess, but that's the care that's going into making this one."

"Lunch break," calls Rydell.

Fonda is quickly out of his chair, into his car, and he'll be first in the chow line right up there with the grips, Mister Roberts still hanging out with his crew.

"Didja ever see anyone like him?" asks one of them. "Always lining up with the rest of us when he could be waited on. I guess that's why we all call him Mister Fonda."

But it is not "Miss Hepburn." She's "Katharine" or "Kate" to all. It's "We're ready, Katharine" or "Would you please stand there, Kate?" She teases a lighting man by boxing with him. She leans on an overalled grip or, talking with him, puts her left arm around the neck of a sound technician. To your astonishment, she's flirtatiously, girlishly tactile, always reaching out, seeming to treat others as extensions of herself, a camaraderie of equals.

Having reviewed scores of her performances, I'd never tried to meet her because she's always suggested to me the chilly grandeur of the nineteenth century's Dowager Empress of China. You can't imagine any of the courtiers referring to the Dowager Empress as Tzu or Hsi or even Tzu Hsi. When a grip called her "Kate," away blew my career-long image of Hepburn as the Dowager Empress of China.

"Yes," she sighs. "Filmmaking is painfully slow, forever waiting around for the setup to be just right, the light from the sky, the lights we carry, the sounds of boats on the lake or cars on the road. But I love it! I'm a morning person, always up by five-thirty and rarin' to go. You adjust. The short takes may seem difficult to pick up, but you put your mind to it and you know where you are.

"Not like the theater at all. Now that's hard, hard work, those three compressed hours. Night after night I sit in my dressing room literally frozen with terror.

"Why can't I ever get used to it? I never can and I'm always terrified. Once it starts, of course, you get going and there's no time to think of anything but what you simply must do.

"I thought that long tour of *Coco* would never end, because, with a big musical like that, you're even more conscious of exactly how many people and their unseen families are relying upon you for a livelihood.

"That's something most people never think of about being a star. The price you pay for it is the constant awareness of how many others are depending on you. It haunts you. Me, anyway. I'm a strict New Englander. You can't be sick. If you break an arm or a leg, you wear a cast and go on anyway as I've done. You always have to be up because if you're down, everyone else is too.

"Isn't this a marvelous setting for the Thayers? This land around here is largely owned by the

Mead family, a big one. Their story goes back to the day the Wrights first flew at Kitty Hawk. Old Mr. Mead, whose widow still lives here, bought the land after inventing the air-cooled engine, which revolutionized aviation."

Katharine now goes into a knowledgeable history of aircraft, how they work and why.

She is told that author Thompson has just taken off for a quick trip to New York. "I told him all the routes to take and he was going to use a different one." She ticks off every turn on both routes. "My way would have saved him probably two hours."

She discusses bouillabaisse, which her chef and hairdresser, Ray Gow, prepared in honor of a dinner party she gave for Shirlee and Henry, "though it's not a favorite of mine," and she rattles off exactly what goes into bouillabaisse, how much, and when.

There is, you think, nothing in this world which doesn't interest this woman and which she hasn't looked into and remembered.

Her face is remarkably unlined, still freckled, and her eyes are more blue than they seem from a distance. She is far smaller, slighter than she seems on stage, and though presently she is suffering from a painful right shoulder, her darting movements give no such indication.

"It was the last set of a three-day spate of tennis with Noel Willman before we came up here. I racketed my shoulder completely out of joint and it was beginning to get better up here when I walked right into a glass door. Now it's in constant pain and I can't move my fingers, which I do want to do for the piano scenes in *The West Side Waltz*, Thompson's new play which Noel will direct and in which I'll make a national tour after we finish filming here. I read a barrel of plays, you can imagine, and I find Thompson far the most able, understanding, and professional of the whole current crop. A perceptive young man. But here I am, can hardly raise my arm, see, but what can you do? You just go on and make the best of it.

"That's why we're here despite the strike. Who knows how we could all get together this time next year? Has to be summer. It took a whale of detailed planning, but this apartness seems promising for what we all sense will be a good film."

Jane Fonda's Chelsea doesn't enter Rydell's shooting schedule until later. She's just arrived from completing *9 to 5* with Lily Tomlin, Dolly Parton, and Elizabeth Wilson. Another member of that cast, and he'll be very much noticed when *9 to 5* opens at Christmas, is Dabney Coleman, here to act Chelsea's dentist friend, Bill.

But already Jane is preparing for a film assignment she's never had: a backflip dive. She practices this several hours a day and also holds those exercise classes she's noted for in Los Angeles.

Joining Jane for them daily are her stepmother, Shirlee, only a few years older than Jane, and actress Patricia McCormack, author Thompson's longtime pal, who's here with her two children—ten-year-old Bobby, and Danielle, nine.

Add to the youth list actor Douglas McKeon,
who's playing Billy.

His canvas chair labeled "Doug McKeon," he's
shooting his scenes early because he must be
back when California's schools open. A sunny-
faced towhead, Doug's been acting for nine of
his fourteen years and has his scenes down with
uncanny concentration. He's all prepared for
that traditional first assignment of any fall term:
"How I Spent My Summer Vacation."

By the final shooting day Fonda will have
used his favorite wind-down hobby, painting, to
create a striking portrait of a hat, a hat once
worn by Spencer Tracy and given to him the
day filming started by Katharine. The original
painting goes to Katharine, but there will be
two hundred copies for all who worked on the
film.

Six months after the New Hampshire filming,
director Rydell will be huddled over his Kem
Bild-Ton System, a sophisticated outcropping
of those old movieolas on which early directors
and editors did their cutting and splicing. His
longtime favorite film editor, Robert Wolfe, will
have died following an illness which heightened
after their return from Big Squam. David Grusin's
scoring will have had a full-scale orchestra tap-
ing in March and, gradually, over the summer,
publicity tom-toms will have begun for one of
1981's most promising films.

By then the year will have seen 150 different
stage productions around the world of *On Golden
Pond* Hepburn will have broken house records

on tour in Thompson's *The West Side Waltz*, Henry Fonda will have opted to appear in his *Answers*, and Thompson will have completed still another play, *A Sense of Humor*.

Remembering the summer day of 1978 when I first read *On Golden Pond*, I hope Thompson still will be pulling plays out of the latest fangled word-processor in 2028. By then, like Norman, at the beginning of the play, he would be seventy-nine.

Arthur Cantor and Greer Garson presented The Hudson Guild Theatre Production, Craig Anderson, Producer, of ON GOLDEN POND *on Wednesday, February 28, 1979, at the New Apollo Theatre, New York City.*

ORMAN THAYER, JR.	*Tom Aldredge*
ETHEL THAYER	*Frances Sternhagen*
CHARLIE MARTIN	*Ronn Carroll*
CHELSEA THAYER WAYNE	*Barbara Andres*
BILLY RAY	*Mark Bendo*
BILL RAY	*Stan Lachow*

Directed by CRAIG ANDERSON
Set Design and Costumes by STEVEN RUBIN
Lighting Design by CRAIG MILLER

ON GOLDEN POND *was first presented by The Hudson Guild Theatre, Craig Anderson, producing director, David Kerry Heefner, associate director; Harold Sogard, managing director, at The Hudson Guild Theatre, New York City, September 13, 1978, for a limited run of 36 performances.*

NORMAN THAYER, JR.	*Tom Aldredge*
ETHEL THAYER	*Frances Sternhagen*
CHARLIE MARTIN	*Ronn Carroll*
CHELSEA THAYER WAYNE	*Zina Jasper*
BILLY RAY	*Mark Bendo*
BILL RAY	*Stan Lachow*

Directed by CRAIG ANDERSON
Set Design and Costumes by STEVEN RUBIN
Lighting Design by CRAIG MILLER
Production Stage Manager, DANIEL MORRIS

ON GOLDEN POND

ACT ONE

SCENE ONE

The middle of May. Early afternoon.

The setting is the living room of a summer home on Golden Pond, in Maine. The room is large and old and high-ceilinged, all wood and glass, not sparkling like a picture in HOUSE BEAUTIFUL, *but rich and wrinkled and comfortable-looking. The house was built in 1914, as a plaque on the chimney proclaims, and it has aged well. Its beams and plank walls are a deep brown, window sills and doorways fading green, hooked rugs and plaid curtains still bright. There is a line of windows upstage, the sort that can be cranked open, with screens on the outside. Through them can be seen trees, and then a brightness because the sun is reflecting on the lake down below. If one looked far enough, one could see mountains in the distance. And that is all. Just a house on a lake in the woods.*

There is a heavy paneled door up right, open now, showing a screen door beyond it, and an outside porch beyond that, a platform really with several outdoor chairs sitting on it. In the left corner up-

stage a stairway leads up to a landing where there
is a closed door, and then bends and rises higher
still, disappearing into a hallway. The upstage
area of the room is raised by two or three steps. In
the right corner is a tall folding glass door, closed
now, and beyond it a dining area, an old oak table
with chairs piled on its top. The stage right wall is
dominated by a huge fieldstone fireplace with a
wide slab hearth. On either side there are wood-
boxes with plaid cushions, and, above them, shelves
and shelves of books and games and knickknacks
and more books, rising all the way to the ceiling.
Stage left there is another, smaller table, chairs
upside down on it, too, and there are two doors,
both closed. The upstage one is the swinging vari-
ety, and the entrance to the kitchen; the downstage
door leads outside. A little window beside it shows a
bit of the shingled back porch and more trees.

The room is a trifle disorganized. Its furniture, a
fat couch, and two fat chairs, two rockers by the
fireplace, are all covered with dust cloths. A chair
by the entrance door has a footstool overturned in
its lap, and, next to it, a small table holding a
fifties-style telephone. There are other tables,
curious handmade relics, clustered in the center of
the room waiting to go outside. The rugs are all
rolled up. There are floor lamps here and there,
end tables, hassocks, a basket of wood, bric-a-brac
galore, fishing poles in a rack, anchors, pine cones,
boat cushions, and the like. A row of old hats and a
pair of binoculars hang from hooks upstage. Everything looks as though it's been there forever,

and while the room is cluttered it still looks like a nice place to curl up and take a nap. Everywhere, on the walls and on the mantel, on the bookshelves and window sills, on the tables and the doors, are pictures, photographs, most of them framed, most of them old and brown, some new. Pictures of people, groups, families, children, animals, places, the whole room a huge photo album, a huge book of memories.

When the curtain rises there is quiet for a moment, and then footsteps can be heard in the hall upstairs. NORMAN THAYER, JR., *appears on the steps. He is 79. He wears baggy pants and sneakers and a sweater. His hair is white. He wears glasses. He walks slowly but upright. On the one hand he is boyish and peppery, having hung onto his vigor and his humor, but at the same time, he is grand, he has a manner, a way of speaking and of carrying himself that seem to belong in another era. It is a larger-than-life quality, an extra dimension of size that old men seem to take on.* NORMAN's *health is good, a touch of arthritis, palpitations, gout, and a few other slight irregularities notwithstanding. He is flirting with senility, but he knows it and he plays it to the hilt.*

He stands on the landing, taking in the room. He smiles. He walks down to the raised platform and stops at the entrance door. He stares out at the lake. He pushes the screen door, but instead of opening, it falls over. NORMAN *watches it smack*

*down onto the porch. He considers it a moment,
then he turns and faces the room again. He studies
it slowly, an old friend. His gaze gets him to the
fireplace and he steps down to it. He takes his time.
He lifts the dust cover on one of the couches and
peers beneath it. He steps to the phone and lifts the
receiver. He listens. He calls offstage.*

NORMAN

The phone works!
>   (*He waits for an answer. There isn't one. He
>   speaks to himself*)

At least I think it does.
>   (*He returns the receiver to its cradle. He stares at
>   the phone. After a moment he picks it up again
>   and listens. He squints and dials "0." He listens. A
>   moment passes*)

Hello? . . . Hello, hello?
>   (*His attention is diverted by a photo propped up on
>   the mantel in front of him. He squints at it*)

Who the hell is that?
>   (*He calls offstage*)

Who the *hell* is in this picture here?
>   (*He waits for a response. There isn't one. He talks
>   to himself*)

Who the hell *is* that?
>   (*A voice has come on the phone*)

Hello? . . . Yes. . . . Yes, hello. . . . Who is
this? . . . The operator! Oh, hello. How are
you? . . . How nice. What do you want? . . . You
called, you must want something. . . . I didn't, you

know. . . . Wait a minute, yes, I *did* call you. But that
was a long time ago. You never answered. . . . I see.
Well, here you are. How *are* you? . . . How nice. Listen, this is Norman Thayer, Jr., over on Golden
Pond. . . . *Golden Pond.* . . . It's in New England,
dear, in the state of Maine. Where are you? . . . I
thought so. You have the accent, you know. . . .
Well, it doesn't matter. Golden Pond is very near
wherever you are. . . . I have something I would like
you to do, if you could. . . . Call me up. Can you do
that? . . . I want to check my phone and make certain it rings. It hasn't been rung all winter, that we
know of. It may have lost its whatsie. . . . Thank
you, dear. Do you have my number? . . . Well, I
should think you would. . . . What do you mean,
written on the phone? There's nothing written on the
phone.

(Staring at the dial)

Oh, wait a minute. I see what you mean. But I can't
make it out. . . .

(He bends closer)

Nope. Sorry. Too small. They should write the numbers bigger. You'll have to look it up, dear. . . . I
haven't a clue. It has a nine in it, that's all I
know. . . . Yes, I suppose there *are* a lot of numbers
with nines. Well, it's in the book. You must have a
book. . . . Norman Thayer, Jr. In the state of
Maine. . . . Fine. . . . Thank you very much.

*(He hangs up. He stares at the phone expectantly.
Nothing happens. He puts his hand on the receiver
in anticipation. A moment passes. Once again he
squints at the photo)*

Who the hell *is* that?

> (*Now there comes a pounding on the downstage
> door.* NORMAN *is startled. He stares for a moment.
> The knock is repeated.* NORMAN *calls offstage*)

Someone's at the door!

ETHEL
(*Offstage*)

It's me, you poop!

> (NORMAN *steps to the door and opens it. In walks*
> ETHEL THAYER, *his wife. She is 69, small, but
> energetic beyond belief. She is* NORMAN's *opposite
> in many ways. She fills the empty spaces when he
> grows quiet. They are best of friends, with a keen
> understanding of each other, after 48 years of
> marriage. She is dressed in rolled-up blue jeans
> and sneakers, a plaid workshirt, and a jacket, a
> bright scarf on her head. She marches to the center
> of the room carrying a basket of branches.* NOR-
> MAN *smiles at her*)

NORMAN

Look at you.

ETHEL
(*Checking herself quickly*)

Yes. Quite a sight, aren't I?

NORMAN

Where have you been?

ETHEL

In the woods.

NORMAN

In the woods. How nice.

ETHEL

Oh! It's *beautiful!* Everything's just waking up. Little tiny birds, little tiny leaves. I saw three little tiny chippies, and a whole patch of little tiny flowers out by the old cellar hole. I forget what they're called, little tiny yellow things. And millions and millions of little tiny black flies. In my eyes and hair. Just terrible!

NORMAN

What were you doing out there in the woods?

ETHEL

Getting kindling.
                    (*She sets it on the hearth*)
That should last us about an hour and a half. Going to be a bit nippy tonight, I'd say. I had a terrible time finding anything dry.
        (*She smiles at him, and then looks about the room*)
Just look at this place.

NORMAN

It's a mess, isn't it?

ETHEL

Not really. Just take a minute and it'll be all shipshape again. Come on. Help me with the dust covers. What's happened to the screen door?

NORMAN

It fell over.

ETHEL

How?

NORMAN

I pushed it.

ETHEL

What do you mean?

NORMAN

I pushed the door and the door fell over.

ETHEL

It's not supposed to do that when you push it.

NORMAN

I didn't think so. I'll fix it later.

ETHEL
(*Crossing to the door*)
You might have closed the big door.

NORMAN

Didn't want to touch it. I was afraid of what might happen.

ETHEL

Well, now we'll be swatting at black flies for the next two days.
(*She closes the door*)
The room is probably full of them.

NORMAN
(*Looking about*)

I don't see any.

ETHEL

You *don't* see them till it's too late.
(*She stares out the window*)
Of course they're never quite as bad on the lake side.
Not when the wind blows. Whitecaps today.

NORMAN

Ah.

ETHEL

(*Crossing back down and beginning another dust
cover*)
I met a very nice couple.

NORMAN

What? Where?

ETHEL

In the woods.

NORMAN

You met a couple in the woods? A couple of people?
(*He is neatly folding his dust cover*)

ETHEL

No, a couple of antelope. Of course a couple of
people. You needn't be too careful with that. I'm
going to hang them out on the line anyway.

NORMAN

Oh.

(He thinks about it for a moment and then continues folding it)

What were these people doing in the woods?

ETHEL

Walking. Their name was Melciorri, I think, or something.

NORMAN

Melciorri? What sort of name is that?

ETHEL

I don't know, dear. Italian, probably. They're up from Boston.

NORMAN

Ohhh. They speak English?

ETHEL

Tsk. Of course they speak English. How do you suppose I talked to them?

NORMAN

You're not fluent in Italian, then?

ETHEL

(Lifting a dust cover)

Here, help me with this. They're a very nice middle-aged couple. Just like us.

NORMAN
(Dropping his own dust cover and taking an end of hers)
If they're just like us, they're not middle-aged.

ETHEL
Of course they are.

NORMAN
Middle age means the middle, Ethel. The middle of life. People don't live to be 150.

ETHEL
We're at the far edge of middle age, that's all.

NORMAN
We're not, you know. We're not middle-aged. You're old, and I'm ancient.

ETHEL
Pooh. You're in your seventies and I'm in my sixties.

NORMAN
Just barely on both counts.

ETHEL
Are we going to spend the afternoon quibbling about this?

NORMAN
We can if you'd like.

ETHEL
(*Picking up another cover*)
The Melciorris, whatever their age group, are a nice
couple, that's all. They're staying up at the Putnams',
while the Putnams are in Europe.

NORMAN
Do the Putnams know about this?

ETHEL
Yes. They're best of friends. That's what Mrs. Melciorri said.

NORMAN
Ha! Ha! Ha!

ETHEL
Oh, Lord. They've invited us for dinner, if we like.

NORMAN
(*Removing the footstool from the chair and setting
it on the floor. He studies with great concern the
stool's decrepit condition*)
Oh. Well. I don't know about that. I'm not sure my
stomach is ready for rigatoni and that sort of thing.

ETHEL
We didn't discuss the menu. Mister Melciorri says he's
a fisherman. Maybe we'd have fish.

NORMAN
Oh.

ETHEL

He says you could go along with him any time you'd
like. Fishing.

NORMAN
(*Not excited*)

Oh.

ETHEL

Wouldn't that be nice? Have someone to fish with?

NORMAN
(*Not excited*)

Yes.

ETHEL

Well. I'll tell Mrs. Melciorri, next time I see her, that
we'd be delighted to come to dinner.

NORMAN
(*Not excited*)

Good.

ETHEL

Now. Let's see what we've got here. Want to help me
with the rugs?
(*She studies the room*)

NORMAN

I don't have anything else to do.

ETHEL

Guess who else I ran into.

NORMAN

You ran into someone else? The woods are full of people. What's this place coming to?

ETHEL

It was only Charlie.

NORMAN

Who's Charlie?

ETHEL

Charlie. The mailman.

NORMAN

Oh. What was Charlie the mailman doing in the woods?

ETHEL

He was on the road.

NORMAN

Oh. You went on the road, too. You didn't say that. You said you were in the woods.

(*They unroll the rugs,* NORMAN *barely helping*)

ETHEL

Well, the road goes through the woods, you know.

NORMAN

Of course it does.

ETHEL

Charlie wants to put in our dock.

NORMAN

What for?

ETHEL

To park the boat beside.

NORMAN

I'll put in the dock.

ETHEL

You *won't* put in the dock.

NORMAN

Why not?

ETHEL

Because you're too old.

NORMAN

I'm not old at all. I'm middle-aged.

ETHEL

Old Pearson's been putting in the dock for God knows how long anyway, but he died this past winter, so Charlie has offered to do it, now that Pearson has received his just reward.

NORMAN

How did that come about?

ETHEL

I don't know. I suppose he got ill.

NORMAN

No, how did the subject of our dock come about?

ETHEL

We started talking about the dock because Charlie said it would be two more weeks before he'd start delivering the mail by boat, and he wanted to be sure we were okay. He must be the busiest man in the state of Maine.

NORMAN

I should think so. Certainly the dimmest-witted.

ETHEL

Norman.

(*She finds a cloth and begins to dust*)

NORMAN

I remember Charlie when he was just a little fellow.

ETHEL

Yes.

NORMAN

Little blond-haired kid. Used to laugh at anything. I thought then that he was a bit deficient. I remember when he used to pass out the mail for his uncle. One time he had a package for us, I remember, a box of salt-water taffy from someone in New Jersey, and he was balancing out there on the deck of that old tub they used to have, and he fell right off and splashed into the lake.

ETHEL

I remember that.

NORMAN

Years ago. I laughed till I thought I'd die. I was sitting down there on the dock, with old Chum, waiting for the paper. I laughed and laughed, and then Chum started to laugh. At least I think that's what he was doing. Remember how he used to bark and it sounded like he was laughing?

(ETHEL *smiles and nods her head*)

Charlie's uncle laughed. The passengers on the boat all laughed. Everyone laughed. This went on for some time, and it suddenly occurred to all of us at once that Charlie hadn't come back·up. I got out of my chair to look for him, figuring he'd probably drowned and we'd never find out what was in the package, and it was then I realized he was under the dock, embarrassed to death and afraid that Chelsea had seen him take his bellyflop.

ETHEL

She had, too. She used to stay in her room and watch him every day when she was a teenager.

NORMAN

Well, I told him she was out in the back on her bicycle, and he finally crawled out and gave me our soggy package. I never liked salt-water taffy anyway. It's always so sticky. It's a stupid thing to eat. I don't know who would have sent us something like that. Some former student who was unhappy with his grades, I expect. Charlie must be thirty by now.

ETHEL

Charlie is forty-four. Two years older than Chelsea.

NORMAN

Chelsea is forty-two? Our Chelsea?

ETHEL

'Fraid so.

NORMAN

Good God.
(NORMAN *is up by the door, studying the rack of hats. A moment passes. He takes down an old straw hat and puts it on. He admires himself in a small mirror that hangs by the door.* ETHEL *puffs up to him with a table*)
What do you think?

ETHEL

Quite a sight.

NORMAN

I should say so. How's the table, a bit heavy?

ETHEL

Lord, yes. My father built this table in 1917, I think. Yes. It's practically as old as the house.
(*She sets it by the door*)

NORMAN

Your *father made* that?

ETHEL
(*Slightly annoyed*)

Yes. The first summer I went to Camp Koochakiyi.
(NORMAN *replaces the hat and dons a new one, a
floppy red fishing hat. He checks himself out
again*)
Charlie says he doesn't expect Miss Appley to make it
up this year.

NORMAN

Who's Miss Appley?

ETHEL

Miss *Appley*, Norman, who lives with Miss Tate.

NORMAN

Ohhh. How do you like this one?

ETHEL

Stunning. They're both in their nineties, I should
think. They were up here together when I was a teenager. Wearing their neckties and singing in the
gazebo, holding hands. What a marvelous love affair,
if that's what it is.

NORMAN

Yes.
(*He's trying on another hat*)

ETHEL

Can you imagine being together for so long?

NORMAN

No.

ETHEL

(*She throws the pile of dust cloths into the kitchen*)
Thanks a lot. Charlie says Miss Appley is just too frail,
and Miss Tate won't come without her. One of them
has a nephew, I believe, who'll get the house. It's sad,
isn't it?
    (*She looks at* NORMAN *quickly and goes on, busy-
    ing herself with dusting*)
Did you see the mouse tracks all over the kitchen?
The little rascals must have had a wonderful winter.

NORMAN

Yes. That's nice, isn't it?

ETHEL

I don't think it's nice at all. It's our house, they have
no right settling in like that.

NORMAN

It's nice to think there was life here. Keeps the house
company, it doesn't get lonely.

ETHEL

Yes. But mice?

NORMAN

They're better than Italians from Boston.
    (*He's put on still another hat, which he'll keep on
    for the rest of the scene*)

ETHEL

Tsk.

> (*She bends over and retrieves a wooden doll that has fallen onto the hearth*)

Oh, poor Elmer has had a terrible fall.

NORMAN

Who's poor Elmer?

ETHEL

Elmer.

> (*She holds up the doll*)

My dolly. He fell in the fireplace.

NORMAN

Oh. How did that happen?

ETHEL

The mice probably. They probably gave him a push just to be nasty. Poor little Elmer. The life you've had.

> (*To* NORMAN)

Did you know he turned sixty-five this spring?

NORMAN

No, I must say I wasn't aware of that.

ETHEL

I got him on my fourth birthday. I remember it quite clearly. I wanted a red scooter, but my father said red scooters were excessive and contrary to the ways of the Lord. He told me I'd understand when I was older. I'm a *lot* older now, and I'm afraid I still don't understand. But, he gave me Elmer. And Elmer and I

became the best of friends. The times we had. He was
my first true love. you know.

NORMAN

There's no real need for you to review the vagaries of
your youth. I've realized all along that I wasn't the
first in line.

ETHEL

No, you were a rather cheap substitute for my darling
Elmer. Sixty-five years old. It's hard to think of a doll
as being old. He doesn't look much different than he
did. A bit faded perhaps. He'd still be a delight to a
small child. Chelsea used to love him. And now he's
had a fall, poor dear.

NORMAN

Maybe he was trying to kill himself. Maybe he wants
to be cremated. Probably got cancer or termites or
something. You know what happens. First . . .

ETHEL
(Interrupting)
Would you please shut up. I swear you get more mor-
bid every year.

NORMAN

Well, it wouldn't be a bad way to go, huh? A quick
front flip off the mantel, a bit of a kick at the last
minute, and land right in the fire. Nothing to it.

ETHEL

Are you hungry, Norman?

NORMAN

Nope. When my number's up, do that for me, would you? Prop me up on the mantel and point out which way is down. I may even shoot for a full gainer with a half twist.

ETHEL

Norman . . .

NORMAN

It's that little kick at the end I might have trouble with. You could get Charlie and hoist me back up again if I make a mess of it.

ETHEL

Norman . . .

NORMAN

Give me three tries and we'll go with the highest score. I'd be pretty well dead anyway after three full gainers with half twists, so if I haven't managed to hit the fire by the third go, you could just give me a bit of a nudge.

ETHEL

Norman, you're not remotely funny.

NORMAN

I think I'll have that written into the final instructions of my will. Let's call up that Jewish person in Wilmington and see how much he'd charge for a rewrite. He'll be delighted to hear about the saving. You won't even need an urn. You can just shovel me out when I'm done and put me on your flowers.

ETHEL

Norman, you really are becoming a nitwit, aren't you?
(*The phone rings*)

NORMAN

That's probably Mr. Shylock now. Wanting to know if
one of us has pooped out yet.

ETHEL

Your fascination with dying is beginning to frazzle my
good humor.
(*The phone rings*)

NORMAN

It's not a fascination. It just crosses my mind now and
then.

ETHEL

Every five minutes. Don't you have anything else to
think about?

NORMAN

Nothing quite as interesting.
(*The phone rings*)

ETHEL

Well, what's stopping you? Why don't you just take
your dive and get it over with? See what it's like.

NORMAN

And leave you alone with Elmer? You must be mad.
There are probably hundreds of Elmers out there
waiting for you to get free. I know all those widow

stories. Do you suppose you're going to answer that phone?

ETHEL

Yes.
>   (*She glowers at him and then crosses and lifts the receiver*)

Hello? . . . Hello?
>   (*To* NORMAN)

There's no one there.

NORMAN

Ah ha!

ETHEL

Hello? . . . Oh, hello. . . . Yes. . . . Just a moment, please.
>   (*She holds the phone out*)

It's for you.

NORMAN
>   (*Stepping down to her*)

Who is it?

ETHEL

I don't know.

NORMAN

Not Saint Peter, is it?
>   (*She shakes her head and stabs him with the phone. She goes upstage and begins cranking open the windows, and perhaps dusting them a bit*)

Hello? . . . Who is this?
> *(To* ETHEL*)*

It's the operator.
> *(Into the phone)*

What do you want? . . . I don't think so. . . . Oh, to
check the ring, of course. I'd given up on you. Does it
work? . . . Yes, I guess it did ring here, come to
think of it. That's why we picked up. . . . Yes. So.
Everything's all hunky dory, then, huh? . . . Great.
Thank you. . . . I beg your pardon? . . . Oh.
Thank you. Bye!
> *(He hangs up and turns to* ETHEL*)*

She said to have a nice day. What a strange thing to
say. What did she think I was going to do? Well, the
phone works.

ETHEL

Good. What about these fish poles? Been through
them this year?

NORMAN

No. I doubt that I'll be doing any fishing this time
round.

ETHEL

All right.

NORMAN

Seems a shame to spend the money for a license.

ETHEL

All right.

NORMAN

You'd think they'd give it free to an old case like me. It's not as though I'd go out there and deplete the entire trout population or anything.

ETHEL

You always catch your share. You always have.

NORMAN

Well, that's all behind me now.

ETHEL

All right, Norman.
(*He looks about. There is tension in the air. He looks at the photo on the mantel*)

NORMAN

Who the *hell* is in this picture?

ETHEL

What picture?

NORMAN

This one. Here. Some fat woman with a little fat boy.

ETHEL

What? Oh. That's Millie's daugher Jane, and her grandson. I can't remember his name.

NORMAN

Oh. Who's Millie?

ETHEL

Millie, Norman. Our next-door neighbor in Wilmington.

NORMAN

Oh, yes. So that's what her name is. Well, there's a certain family resemblance through the generations, isn't there? Everyone's fat.

> (ETHEL *laughs.* NORMAN *looks about on the mantel*)

Look. Here's Chelsea on the swim team at school. She wasn't exactly thin.

ETHEL

She had a few fat years.

NORMAN

It's no wonder she couldn't do a back flip. No center of gravity.

ETHEL

Well, she tried, Norman.

NORMAN

Oh, of course she did. I remember.

ETHEL

She only did it for you anyway. She only wanted to please you.

NORMAN

Yep.

ETHEL

Maybe this year we could persuade her to come and spend a few days. Wouldn't that be nice?

(*A moment passes.* NORMAN *breaks the mood*)

NORMAN

Feel like a quick game of Parcheesi?

ETHEL

Not right this minute.

NORMAN

Okay.

(ETHEL *goes about cleaning and opening windows*)

I guess you wouldn't be up for Monopoly either then, huh?

ETHEL

Tonight, Norman.

(*She smiles*)

We've got the whole summer. The whole summer for you to try and win back the fortunes you lost to me last year.

NORMAN

Heh heh.

ETHEL

I hope you've thought about your tactics over the winter.

(*She goes on with her work. He pulls down a book and settles into a chair*)

NORMAN

Heh heh.

ETHEL

Pretty shoddy, some of those moves of yours.
(*She hasn't noticed him sitting*)

NORMAN

Heh heh.

(*He gets comfortable*)

ETHEL

We've got the whole summer. But right now I think
we ought to get this place in order, before we start
lolling around.
(NORMAN *puts down his book guiltily. He stands*)
Why don't you read a book or something? Be com-
fortable.
(*He lowers himself back into the chair*)
Unless you feel like helping me.
(*Again he puts down his book and stands.* ETHEL
has never turned around)
But that's all right. There's really nothing for you to
do.
(*He stands still for a moment. Then sits. A moment
passes.* ETHEL *is at the last window, looking out at
the lake*)
It's so good to be home, isn't it?

NORMAN
(*Reading at last*)

Mmmm.

ETHEL
(*Quite loudly*)

Norman!

NORMAN
(*Dropping his book*)

What?

ETHEL

Come here, quick!

NORMAN
(*Going as quickly as he can*)
What on earth is it? Not your heart?

ETHEL

The loons, Norman! I've spotted the loons!

NORMAN

Where?

ETHEL

Get the glasses. My word!
(NORMAN *fetches the binoculars off their hook and
stands beside* ETHEL. *He trains them on the lake*)
They're so lovely. Do you see them?

NORMAN

No. Oh. Oh, my goodness. There they are.

ETHEL

Aren't they lovely?

NORMAN

They're huge! I've never seen such big loons in my life!

ETHEL
(*Looking at where he's aimed the binoculars*)
Those are boats, you poop. Come in closer. By the float.

NORMAN
(*Lowering the glasses*)
Oh. Those little things. Look at them swimming about.

ETHEL

Black and sleek. Lovely animals.

NORMAN

How wonderful.

ETHEL

A husband and a wife. I think they're looking at us.

NORMAN

Yes, they are.

ETHEL

Oh, Norman, they're nudging each other. They're talking.

NORMAN

Yes. But I can't make out what they're saying.
(*He passes her the binoculars*)
Can you read beaks?

ETHEL
(Looking through the glasses)
They're kissing is what they're doing.

NORMAN
How wonderful.

ETHEL
Mmmm.
(She giggles. A moment passes as they stare out at the lake. NORMAN puts his arm around ETHEL. She smiles up at him)
Do you realize this is our forty-eighth summer together, Norman? Our forty-eighth summer on Golden Pond.

NORMAN
Huh.
(After a moment)
Probably be our last.

ETHEL
Oh, shut up.
(They stand together without moving, gazing out the window)

SCENE TWO

The middle of June. Mid-morning.

The setting is the same. The room looks more lived in: there are several vases of flowers, a tablecloth on the oak table, a pile of newspapers by one of the couches, little additions. The windows are all open, the big door closed. The little tables are on the porch now, the screen door is back in place.

NORMAN is sitting in his chair, studying the classified ads with a magnifying glass. He wears the same baggy trousers, a different sweater. His hat is back on the rack. After a moment he looks up and calls offstage.

NORMAN
Here's one. Listen. "Driver wanted for occasional chauffeuring and errands. Five days a week. Pay negotiable." Sound about right?
　　(He waits for an answer. There is none. He reads on to himself)
"Experience required." Well, I guess I've had experience. I've driven enough cars, God knows.
　　　　(He calls offstage)

How many cars would you say I've had?
>   (*No answer. He talks to himself*)
Twenty probably. If you don't count the Nash.
Twenty cars and one Nash. Sounds like experience to
me. God knows I've done my share of errands.
>   (*He calls*)
I think I'll give these people a call. Huh?
>   (*No answer. Then, to himself*)
There's no number. How do you like that? For God's
sake. It's so typical. They want a man for a job and yet
they don't list the number. Well, I hope those errands
weren't too crucial. Good God!
>   (*He reads on. There is a knock on the door.* NOR-
>   MAN *looks up, startled. He stands and walks to-*
>   *ward the porch door. The knock is repeated. He*
>   *stops and looks downstage. He calls to the kitchen*)
Someone's at the door!

ETHEL
>   (*Offstage*)
It's me, you poop! Open up!
>   (NORMAN *steps down and opens the door.* ETHEL
>   *walks in, a bucket in each hand. She wears the*
>   *same, or similar, jeans, and now has on a sweat-*
>   *shirt.* NORMAN *closes the door behind her*)

NORMAN
What were you doing out there?

ETHEL
I was picking berries. There are oodles and oodles of
little tiny strawberries along the old town road. Look.

NORMAN
(*Looking into the buckets*)
Ah. Very nice.

ETHEL
Unfortunately there are also oodles and oodles of mosquitoes. Worse this year than ever.

NORMAN
Really. I hadn't noticed them.

ETHEL
You've barely gone outside. What on earth you're doing in here on a day like this is beyond me.

NORMAN
Oh. Well. I've been quite busy. I've been looking through yesterday's paper for gainful employment.
(*He crosses to his papers*)

ETHEL
Here we go again.
(*She exits into the kitchen.* NORMAN *doesn't notice her absence*)

NORMAN
Very good prospects, I think. Chauffeurs, yardwork. The Dairy Divine wants an ice-cream dipper. I think I could do something like that, don't you?
(*He turns. She's not there*)
Oh.
(*He looks about him.* ETHEL *walks back into the room*)
Oh. There you are. What do you think?

ETHEL

I think this business of looking in the classified ads is about the silliest lot of nonsense I've ever heard. What are you going to do if you call up, and someone says, "Come on over and start tomorrow"?

NORMAN

Go on over and start tomorrow.

ETHEL

Oh, for the love of God. Whatever is the matter with you? Why don't you take a bucket and go pick us another quart of strawberries? I'll fix us up a scrumptious shortcake for lunch.

NORMAN

You want *me* to pick strawberries?

ETHEL

Yes. Do I have to put an ad in the paper?

NORMAN

I'm not sure I know how to pick strawberries.

ETHEL

There's really nothing to it, Norman. You bend over, and you pick them.

NORMAN

Bend over? Whatever for? Where are they?

ETHEL

They're on the ground, where they belong.

NORMAN

On the ground? Last time we picked blueberries they were on a bush. Didn't have to bend over at all.

ETHEL

Well, these are strawberries, and they don't grow on bushes. They grow on the ground.

NORMAN

No!

ETHEL

'Fraid so. Think you can do it?

NORMAN

I'm sure I could. Do you really want me to?

ETHEL

I insist on it.

NORMAN

But, you've already filled the buckets.

ETHEL

Don't move.
> (*He doesn't. She exits into the kitchen. The sound of a motorboat can be heard.* NORMAN *looks to the lake*)

NORMAN

Here comes whatshisname. He'll be bringing the paper, you know. I wouldn't want to miss any career opportunities just because I'm out looking for strawberries.

ETHEL
(*Coming back with an empty bucket*)
I'll pay you, Norman. It could be the beginning of
something big. You may become a major strawberry
picker

NORMAN
Not if I have to be bending over all the time. I think
you're trying to kill me.

ETHEL
I've thought about it.

NORMAN
You needn't bother. I'm on borrowed time as it is.

ETHEL
Would you please take your cheery personality and
get out of here?

NORMAN
I hope you'll be prepared to massage my bent back
this evening.
(*She steps to him and kisses him*)

ETHEL
With pleasure.

NORMAN
Maybe I could lie down to pick the berries.

ETHEL
Would you go on?
(*He heads for the door, stops and turns*)

NORMAN

Where did you say these strawberries were? Other than on the ground, I mean.

ETHEL

On the old town road. Just up from the meadow.

NORMAN

Oh. Bye!

(*He exits.* ETHEL *watches him go. There's a look in her eyes, partly concern, partly pleasure at making old* NORMAN *get moving. She closes the door and crosses the room, tidies the pile of newspapers. The motor is very loud now.* ETHEL *steps up onto the platform and looks down at the lake. She opens the wooden door and calls through the screen*)

ETHEL

Yoo hoo! Charlie! Hey!

(*The motor stops*)

Good morning. Got some coffee on, if you'd like. Come on up, you can take five minutes off. I'll write you a note and you can send it to the Postmaster General.

(*She steps quickly to the kitchen where she can be heard banging about. After a moment* CHARLIE MARTIN *appears on the porch. He's a big, round, blond-haired man, weatherbeaten face, smiling eyes, strong Maine accent. He is indeed a laugher, but not exactly "deficient." In his own rustic, simple, thoughtful way, he is actually quite charming. He carries a small package, a rolled newspaper,*

*and several letters. He peers through the screen
door)*

CHARLIE

Morning, Ethel.

ETHEL
(*Opening the kitchen door and leaning out*)
Come in, Charlie, and have a seat. Like a biscuit?

CHARLIE

Sure.
(*She goes back inside.* CHARLIE *pulls the screen
door. It falls back over on him. He wrestles with it
and it slams down onto the porch*)
Uh oh.
(ETHEL *comes back out, having heard the noise*)
I think I broke your door.

ETHEL

Oh, no. It's been that way for a month now. I should
have warned you. Norman is supposed to fix it. It's
not high on his list of priorities, I'm afraid.

CHARLIE
(*He sets down the mail and leans the door up
against the wall*)
I could give it a try. It's just missing its little thing-
amabobbers, that's all.

ETHEL

No, better let Norman get to it. Come in and let's close

the big door before every mosquito in the county
finds its way in here.

(*He steps in, laughing, leaving the mail outside*)

CHARLIE

Pretty bad this year, huh?

ETHEL

Worse than ever. Sit down. I'll be right there.

(*She exits.* CHARLIE *looks about and then studies
the chairs before deciding on one and sitting.*
ETHEL *calls from the kitchen*)

How's your brother? We haven't seen him at all this
season.

CHARLIE

You mean Tom?

ETHEL

(*Offstage*)

That's the only brother you have, isn't it?

CHARLIE

Yes. He's fine. He's just come back up from Portland.
Got stopped twice for speeding. Once down and once
up.

(*He laughs his deep, warm laugh*)

By the same policeman.

(*He laughs.* ETHEL *comes in with a tray holding a
coffee percolator and two cups, a plate of biscuits.
She sets them on the table*)

You should have seen his face.

(*He laughs and laughs.* ETHEL *looks at him and
smiles. She pours the coffee and sits across from
him*)

ETHEL

I love your laugh, Charlie.

CHARLIE

Thank you.
                    (*He laughs*)
Tom wasn't too happy to hear it yesterday. I don't
know, it just struck me as awfully funny that he could
be stupid enough to be stopped twice by the same cop.
When he told me, I couldn't stop laughing.
                    (*He laughs*)
Tom's not speaking to me anymore now.
        (*He helps himself to his coffee and grabs a biscuit.*
        ETHEL *smiles at him*)
Where's Norman?

ETHEL

Norman is off picking strawberries. I threw him out.
                (CHARLIE *laughs*)
Don't laugh.
                (CHARLIE *stops*)
Norman is restless this year. I don't know what's got
into him. How's your mother?

CHARLIE

My mother?

ETHEL

Yes.

CHARLIE

She's holding her own.
                (*He laughs and laughs*)
She fell down, you know, a couple of months ago.

ETHEL

I didn't know that.

CHARLIE

Yuh, a couple of months ago, right on her rump,
when she was out helping clean up the town common
with Ladies' Auxiliary. She was having a tug-a-war
with a dead juniper bush, and she won, or lost, depending on how you look at it.

(*He laughs*)

She hasn't been normal since.

(*He laughs*)

She walks all right, and sleeps and everything. She
just can't sit.

(*He snickers*)

It's taken a little adjustment.

(*He laughs and laughs. ETHEL smiles*)

If you'll pardon the expression, though, she's one old
lady who really believes in busting her ass for the
community.

(*He howls, ETHEL joins in. They both roar with
laughter. The downstage door opens and NORMAN
steps in, looking a bit pale, and carrying his
bucket. He stares at ETHEL and CHARLIE. They
both notice him*)

Hi, Norman.

ETHEL

Hello, Norman.

(*She and CHARLIE begin to laugh again. NORMAN
takes on a rather unpleasant look*)

What are you doing back already? You've barely left.

NORMAN

So? I moved fast.
(*He walks toward the kitchen*)
I ran all the way, picked without stopping, and ran all the way back.

ETHEL
(*Rising and starting to head him off*)
Well, I don't believe a word of it. Let me see what you've got.

NORMAN

I'll just dump them in with yours. Stay where you are.

ETHEL
(*Getting closer*)
Let me see.

NORMAN

No. I don't have many.

ETHEL
(*On him now. She reaches for the bucket*)
Just let me see.
(*He tries to pull away. They wrestle with the bucket, it drops on the floor and bounces*)
There's nothing in it at all. You didn't get a single strawberry. What's the matter with you?

NORMAN
(*Looking at the empty bucket*)
I must have eaten them all.

ETHEL

Why didn't you stay and pick some?

NORMAN

Too many mosquitoes. You were right about them. I was afraid I'd contract malaria and die before my time.

ETHEL

Well, I don't know.
(*She picks up the bucket and looks at* NORMAN. *There is a brief uncomfortable moment*)
Do you want some coffee?

NORMAN

No.
(*He looks at* CHARLIE)
No mail today, Charlie?

CHARLIE

Holy Mackinoly! I left it on the porch!

NORMAN

Well, how about bringing it in? Could you do that?

CHARLIE

You bet.
(*He jumps up and goes out the door*)

NORMAN

Look out for the mosquitoes.

ETHEL

You want a glass of milk, Norman?

NORMAN

No.

ETHEL

I'll get you one.
> (*She exits into the kitchen.* NORMAN *watches her
> go. He looks out at* CHARLIE)

NORMAN

I see you broke the screen door, Charlie.

CHARLIE
> (*Coming back in*)

Yuh, well, I think you need a couple of little thing-
amabobbers for the hinges.

NORMAN

Oh, I don't know about that. It's been working all
right. You must have yanked at it.

CHARLIE

The Sander brothers probably left them off when
they put your screens on. I could bring you a couple
from town tomorrow.

NORMAN

Naw. Just be careful next time. Let's have the mail.

CHARLIE

Oh, yuh.
> (*Holding it out*)

Got a package for you.

NORMAN
(*Taking the pile*)
Not salt-water taffy, is it?
(CHARLIE *laughs and laughs*)
You remember that, Charlie?
(CHARLIE *laughs and laughs*)
I guess you do.
(ETHEL *comes back in with a glass of milk*)

ETHEL
Here, Norman. Sit down and drink this.
(*She hands it to him*)

NORMAN
Thank you, nurse.

ETHEL
Tsk. Sit down, Charlie.

CHARLIE
I should get going, I guess. Or somebody's not going
to get their mail.

NORMAN
He's right, Ethel. Neither rain nor sleet nor hot biscuits, and all that.

ETHEL
Sit down, Charlie, and finish your coffee.
(CHARLIE *hesitates and then sits by* NORMAN.
ETHEL *returns to her chair.* NORMAN *is wrestling
with the package*)

CHARLIE

I've only got the Putnams left and three other places, plus the boarding camps.

ETHEL

Have the Putnams heard from the Melciorris at all? Do you know?

CHARLIE

You know, they had a card from them from overseas somewhere. I forget now.

NORMAN

Sicily, I imagine. Ever had white perch cacciatore, Charlie?

CHARLIE

No.

NORMAN

You're a lucky man.

ETHEL

It wasn't that bad. What have you got there, Norman?

NORMAN

I have no idea, I can't open it.
               (*He passes it to* CHARLIE)
Here, could you bite this, please?
       (CHARLIE *laughs, and rips off the cover. He hands
       the box back to* NORMAN, *who squints at it*)

ETHEL

What is it?

NORMAN

I still don't know.

ETHEL

Oh. It's your medicine.

NORMAN

Oh, goody. What a swell surprise.

ETHEL

Just in time. You'd nearly run out.
            (*To* CHARLIE)
It's nothing serious. Just for his palpitations.

NORMAN

Yes, Charlie, I have occasional heart throbs.
        (CHARLIE *laughs.* NORMAN *goes through the three
        or four envelopes*)
Look at this. A bill from Gas and Power in Wilmington, and we're not even there.

ETHEL

It's only a little bit each month.

NORMAN

        (*Thrusting the letter at* CHARLIE)
Here, give this back to them.
        (ETHEL *holds out her hand and* CHARLIE *passes it
        on to her*)
Since you're playing mailman, why don't you just de-
liver all of this to that old lady down there?
        (*He hands the other mail to* CHARLIE, *who laughs
        and passes it to* ETHEL)

I've got to see what's happening in the world. I need
some touch with reality.

> (*He unfolds the paper;* ETHEL *looks through the
> envelopes*)

ETHEL

Ah! A letter from Chelsea.

> (*She opens it eagerly*)

CHARLIE

I noticed that. How is she?

> (*No one answers.* NORMAN *is studying the paper,*
> ETHEL *digs into the long letter*)

Norman?

NORMAN

What?

CHARLIE

Chelsea.

NORMAN

Who?

CHARLIE

Your daughter, Chelsea.

NORMAN

What about her?

CHARLIE

How is she?

NORMAN

Oh. Forty-two.

CHARLIE

What?
                    (*He laughs*)
How *is* she?

NORMAN

Oh. I don't know. You'd have to ask her mother.

CHARLIE

Ethel?

ETHEL

Mmmm.

CHARLIE

How is she?

ETHEL

Mmm-mm.

CHARLIE
    (*Turning back to* NORMAN, *who has opened the
    sports section*)
Is she really forty-two? Norman?

NORMAN

Who?

CHARLIE

Is Chelsea really forty-two?

NORMAN

That's what her mother says.

CHARLIE

Holy Mackinoly. And she went all the way through and never had kids, huh?

NORMAN

What? What do you mean, all the way through?

CHARLIE

Her childbearing years.

NORMAN

Oh. Yes, I suppose so.

CHARLIE

Hmmm.

ETHEL

She sounds like she's having the best time.

CHARLIE

That's great.

NORMAN

Look at the goddam Red Sox.

CHARLIE

Where's she writing from? I couldn't make out the postmark.

NORMAN

What?

CHARLIE

Where's Chelsea writing from?

NORMAN

Home.

CHARLIE
(*Laughing*)

I figured that. Where's she live now?

NORMAN

At home. Goddam Yankees.

ETHEL
(*Not looking up*)

On the coast.

CHARLIE

Oh.

NORMAN

Better tell him which coast, or he'll think she's living
in Bar Harbor. It's California, Charlie.

CHARLIE
(*Laughing*)

I knew that.

ETHEL

He knew that.

NORMAN

Goddam those Orioles. Baltimore has always been a
sneaky town.

ETHEL

Oh, Norman, she says she's coming for your birthday.

NORMAN
(*Looking up*)

Really? How nice.

ETHEL

Yes, and she's bringing her friend.
(*To* CHARLIE)
She has the nicest boyfriend.

CHARLIE

Oh.

(*He half laughs*)

NORMAN

Why?

ETHEL

They're coming together and then they're going on to
Europe for awhile.

NORMAN

Ohhh. Well, I don't want crowds of people here on
my birthday. I don't want crowds of people watching
me turn older.

ETHEL

Oh, pooh. There'll be just the three of us. Is three a
crowd?

NORMAN

That's what they say.

CHARLIE

That's right. Three's a crowd.
(*He laughs*)
What happened to her husband?

ETHEL

Wait a minute. It's not that Freddie person. This is a different boyfriend altogether.

NORMAN

What the hell is going on? Detroit has disappeared. It's gone completely. Good God!

ETHEL

What is it, Norman?

NORMAN

Detroit is gone. Three weeks ago they looked like a contender, and now this stupid paper has them missing.
(*To* CHARLIE)
Do you suppose they've been dropped from the league?
(CHARLIE *shrugs*)
With that stupid commissioner, anything is possible.

CHARLIE

What happened to her husband?

ETHEL
(*Reading*)
Oh, my goodness.

NORMAN
(*Reading*)

What?

ETHEL
(*Looking up*)

What did you say, Charlie?

CHARLIE

I wondered what happened to Chelsea's husband.

ETHEL

He didn't work out.

NORMAN

He couldn't tell the difference between a Negro and an Italian.

CHARLIE

What?

NORMAN

The stupid commissioner. Talking about the so-called greats of the century, and he's got DiMaggio mixed up with Henry Aaron.

ETHEL
(*Reading*)

Oh, my goodness.

NORMAN

That's a pretty hard mistake to make. Good thing he wasn't in charge during the war. He would have invaded Newark in search of Mussolini.

(CHARLIE *laughs*)

That wasn't a joke, Charlie.
> (CHARLIE *stops laughing*)

ETHEL
(*Looking up*)
She says she's in love. With a dentist.

NORMAN
Oh, really? Does her boyfriend know about this?

ETHEL
That is her boyfriend. Her new boyfriend is a dentist.

CHARLIE
That's interesting.

NORMAN
That's who she's bringing here? A dentist?

ETHEL
Yes!

CHARLIE
Huh.

NORMAN
Oh, God. He'll be staring at our teeth all the time.
Why does she have such a fascination with Jewish
people?

ETHEL
Who said this one was Jewish?

NORMAN

He's a dentist, isn't he? Name me one dentist who isn't Jewish.

ETHEL

Your brother.

NORMAN

My brother is deceased. Name me one living dentist who isn't Jewish.

ETHEL

Um . . . I can't think of one offhand.

NORMAN

You see.

CHARLIE

Doctor Baylor.

NORMAN

Who is Doctor Baylor?

CHARLIE

My dentist.

NORMAN

He's in Maine, Charlie. There are no Jews in Maine.

ETHEL

Tsk.

CHARLIE

Sure there are. The Gittelmans over in Spruce Cove.

NORMAN
Those are tourists. Most tourists are Jewish.

CHARLIE
I know a Jewish guy who isn't a tourist. He runs a used-car lot up in Augusta.

NORMAN
I'll bet he does. But, he's obviously an immigrant. From New Jersey or somewhere. There are no native Jews in Maine. Just as there are no native Negroes here, or Puerto Ricans.

ETHEL
I wouldn't think so.

NORMAN
I'm just pointing out to Charlie some of the charms of his habitat. Some of the reasons why we like it so well.
(*To* CHARLIE)
We don't come here just for the bugs, you know.
(CHARLIE *laughs*)
It's true you have your French Canadians, but at least they speak French. So, it's not quite so bad. Makes them sound intelligent.

ETHEL
(*To* CHARLIE)
Oh, Lord. Norman is on a tirade, I'm afraid.
(*To* NORMAN)
This particular dentist who's coming to celebrate your birthday is named Ray, and that doesn't sound Jewish.

NORMAN

It would depend on the last name, I'd say.

ETHEL

That is his last name.

NORMAN

His last name is Ray?

ETHEL

Yes. Bill Ray.

NORMAN

Bill Ray. That sounds rather flippant.

ETHEL

Well, shall we ask him not to come?

NORMAN

No. I think we should have representatives from all
walks of life here for my last birthday party.

ETHEL

Oh, God.
          (*Then, to* CHARLIE, *brightly*)
I think this medicine should be put away from all this
hot air.
      (*She carries it to the kitchen.* NORMAN *glowers
      after her, then turns his stare onto* CHARLIE)

NORMAN

Why didn't you marry Chelsea?

CHARLIE

You wouldn't let me.

NORMAN

Oh.
(*He thinks about it*)
You could have married someone else. I would have
allowed that.

CHARLIE

I didn't want anyone else. I mean, I've come close.
There's still time.

NORMAN
(*Going back to his paper*)
Oh, yes. You've got lots of time.

CHARLIE

How old will you be?

NORMAN

When?

CHARLIE

On your birthday.

NORMAN

One hundred and three.

CHARLIE

Really?
(*He laughs*)
You're kidding. Miss Appley was ninety-seven in May.
Isn't that amazing?

NORMAN
(*Not impressed*)

Yes.

(*He turns to the classified ads*)

CHARLIE

She died, you know.

NORMAN

No.

CHARLIE

Yup. Last Tuesday. We got a call. In case any mail came up.

NORMAN

They gave you a forwarding address for Miss Appley?
(CHARLIE *laughs.* ETHEL *comes back in*)

ETHEL

Now what's going on here?

NORMAN

One of the lesbians expired.
(CHARLIE *roars at this*)

ETHEL

Oh, Norman.
(*To* CHARLIE)

Which one?

CHARLIE

Miss Appley.

ETHEL

Oh, dear. Well, she had a good, full life.

NORMAN

Charlie says she was ninety-seven.

ETHEL

Really? How wonderful.

NORMAN

Puts us all to shame, doesn't it? There's something to
be said for a deviant life style.

CHARLIE

I always liked those old ladies. But I sure used to
wonder what the heck was going on in there.
            (*He stands*)
Well, thanks for the coffee and the biscuits.

ETHEL

Any time, Charlie. You must come round when
Chelsea's here.

CHARLIE

Oh, yuh.
            (*He half laughs*)
I haven't seen her for a long time. Must be . . . well,
let's see. It was the summer my father died, and I was
thirty-six at the time. I'm forty-four now, so
that's. . . .
            (*He figures in his head*)

NORMAN

Eight years.

CHARLIE

Eight years. Holy Mackinoly. Time flies. Well, see you tomorrow.

ETHEL

Okay, dear.
> (*They both look at* NORMAN, *who is engrossed in his paper*)

Norman, Charlie's leaving.

NORMAN

Good.
> (*He looks up*)

Bye!

CHARLIE

Goodbye, Norman.

NORMAN

Watch out for that screen door.

ETHEL
> (*To* CHARLIE)

He really is a poop, isn't he?
> (CHARLIE *laughs, and exits out the big door and across the porch.* ETHEL *closes the door and then calls to him*)

Seen our loons out there today?

CHARLIE
> (*Offstage*)

Yup. Out by Honey Island. They're teaching their baby to fly.

ETHEL

Oh. How exciting. I hope they bring him over to introduce us. Bye, Charlie.

CHARLIE
(*Offstage*)

Bye!

ETHEL

Isn't that exciting? Teaching their baby to fly. Norman? Isn't it exciting?

NORMAN

Mmmm. Listen to this. "Elderly gentleman wanted for companionship and conversation, for convalescing invalid. Three afternoons a week." Now, doesn't that sound perfect?

ETHEL

Perfect for you. I wouldn't have much hope for the invalid.

NORMAN

There's another one here. "Retired people sought for handbill delivery. Mornings or evenings. Some walking involved." I should call, I can walk.

ETHEL

Yes. I can just see you walking out there with those mosquitoes. You'd be eaten alive.

NORMAN

I could carry my screen door with me.

ETHEL

Is that why you came rushing back here? To read those silly ads?.

NORMAN

Could be. Maybe I should have asked Charlie if he needs another man on the boat. I could balance out there on the deck, and fall off at every dock we came to. Could be a source of amusement all around the lake. Be a great boon to the Postal Department. Get more people writing letters. What do you suppose Charlie would pay me?

ETHEL

Whatever is the matter with you? Why do you need a job? You've always loved being here on Golden Pond with nothing to do. Why is this summer any different?

NORMAN

I'm in the market for a last hurrah.

ETHEL

Tsk. Lord. Why can't you just pick berries and catch fish and read books, and enjoy this sweet, sweet time?

NORMAN
(After a pause)

Do you want to know why I came back so fast with my little bucket? I got to the end of our lane, and I . . . couldn't remember where the old town road was. I went a little way into the woods, and nothing looked familiar, not one tree. And it scared me half to death. So I came running back here, to you, to see your

pretty face, and to feel that I was safe. That I was still
me.

> (*He takes off his glasses, and puts his face in his
> hands.* ETHEL *is quite shocked by his speech, but
> she rallies quickly. She bends over him and rubs his
> back*)

ETHEL

Well, you're safe, you old poop. And you're definitely
still you. Still picking on poor Charlie. After lunch,
after we gobble up all the strawberries, I'll *take* you
down to the old town road. You'll remember it all, my
darling, we've walked it a thousand thousand times.
And we'll pick us another batch of those little tiny
berries. And I'll do the bending. You just talk away
the mosquitoes.

> (*She rubs his back, and smiles down at him, sadly*)

SCENE THREE

The middle of July. Early evening.

It is just the edge of darkness; there is still a soft glow in the sky. The room looks quite cheery. A large poster hangs on the stage right wall. It reads: HAPPY BIRTHDAY, NORMAN. *There are several balloons flung about. As the scene progresses and it grows darker outside, little lights may be visible in the distance, other cottages.*

After a moment, ETHEL *enters from the kitchen, carrying another poster. She wears jeans again, and a sweater now. She looks about for a place to put the sign. She crosses to the mantel and props it against the chimney. It says:* WELCOME HOME, CHELSEA. *She looks at it, pleased. She looks about the room. Suddenly she rushes up to the porch door, which is open, the screen back in place. She speaks to the door.*

ETHEL

Get away, you nasty things. Tsk.
       (She waves her hands)
Get off the door!
       (She slaps the screen door)

Get off, go on!
> (*She slaps the door harder. It falls over and onto the porch*)

Oh, Norman, for God's sake!
> (*She screams quietly*)

Acch! Get away, get away, get away!
> (*She quickly closes the big door, and leans against it*)

Worse this year than ever.
> (*She cranks closed one of the windows.* NORMAN *appears on the stairs. He is dressed quite nattily in slacks and shirt, a bright "scenic" tie, and a cardigan sweater. He pauses on the landing*)

NORMAN

Whatever is going on down here?

ETHEL

You and your screen door. The *moths* are trying to get in. I swear you're on their side.

NORMAN

They're just trying to crash my party. It's expected to be the social highlight of the summer season, you know.

ETHEL
> (*Looking up at him*)

My, my, look at you. You have on a tie.

NORMAN
> (*Looking down*)

Yes, I know. I put it there. Do you think I've over-dressed?

ETHEL

I think I'm going to have to do some mighty fast
maneuvers to catch up with you.

NORMAN

I have other ties. You could come as Miss Appley.

ETHEL

Thank you.

NORMAN
(*Looking at his sign*)
You've really outdone yourself with all this.
(*He looks to the fireplace*)
"Welcome home, Chelsea." I see my birthday wasn't
cause enough for a celebration.

ETHEL

Tsk. I just want our little girl to feel welcome.

NORMAN

Ah. Did you know our little girl has passed through
her childbearing years without bearing any children?

ETHEL

Of course I know that. She chose not to, is all.

NORMAN

Hmmm. Seems odd, doesn't it?
(*He comes down the steps*)
Did you ever have that woman-to-woman chat with
her you said you were going to? Maybe she didn't
know how.

ETHEL

Yes, I told her how. Twenty-five years ago. She
seemed to know what I was talking about.

NORMAN

Maybe I should have taken that husband of hers
aside. He seemed like he could have used a few tips.
I've never known anyone so timid in my life.

ETHEL

Every poor soul she's brought home has been timid
around you. You attack them so.

NORMAN

I don't, you know.

ETHEL

Mm-hmm.
            (*Pointedly*)
Wouldn't it be nice if we could all get along this time?

NORMAN

Oh, sure.

ETHEL

I wonder whom I could talk to to arrange that sort of
thing.

NORMAN

Tsk. I intend to be the perfect host. I'll overwhelm
them with my charm.

ETHEL

Mm-hmm. That's what I'm afraid of.

NORMAN
(*He looks about*)
Well. . . . Why aren't they here? I'm getting older by the minute.

ETHEL
They said they'll be here when they get here.

NORMAN
Is that what they said? That's a hell of an attitude. No wonder we have no grandchildren.

ETHEL
What would we do with grandchildren?

NORMAN
Toss them on our knees. We're the last of the Thayers, you know. End of the line for a damn good name.

ETHEL
Well, we'll take it out in style. Shhh.
(*From the lake can be heard the plaintive call of the loon*)
Norman, the loons.
(*The call is repeated. She peers out the window*)
They're calling. Oh, why is it so dark?

NORMAN
Because the sun went down.

ETHEL
I wish I could see them. The baby's gotten so big.
(*She calls*)

Yoo hoo! Looo-ooons!
>   (NORMAN *smiles at her*)
Loony looo-ooons!

NORMAN

I don't think you should do that in front of Chelsea's
companion.

ETHEL

Oh, pooh. I'm just talking to my friends.
>   (*She calls again*)
Yoo hooo!
>   (*Now there is the sound of a car in the back of the
>   the house*)
Oh, no! They're here! And I'm not dressed!

NORMAN

You look dressed.

ETHEL

Oh, no, I wanted to look nice. I look like an old
character.

NORMAN

Run upstairs and change, if it makes you feel better.
I'll stay here and entertain them. I'll make them feel
welcome.

ETHEL

Will you be nice to them?

NORMAN

Sure. I'll explain to them the risk involved in arriving late for an old man's birthday party.

(*The downstage door opens and* CHELSEA THAYER WAYNE *steps in. She is quite pretty, a bit heavy, athletic-looking, tan, a nervous type, something dark about her, but she has her father's humor. She wears slacks and a jersey, basic traveling clothes. She rushes to* ETHEL)

CHELSEA

Mommy.

(*They embrace. Quite intensely.* CHELSEA *looks up to* NORMAN, *who hasn't moved. She steps to him, and hugs him, awkwardly. He is embarrassed, surprised. He hesitates only the briefest instant, then hugs* CHELSEA)

Hello, Norman. Happy birthday.

NORMAN

Look at you.

(*He is touched*)

Look at this little fat girl, Ethel.

CHELSEA

(*Stepping back. She checks herself, embarrassed*)

Oh, yes. I was going to lose it all and show up skinny, but I was afraid you wouldn't recognize me.

ETHEL

You're thin as a rail. Isn't she, Norman?

NORMAN
Yes.

(There follows a moment of adjustment. Nothing is said. ETHEL jumps in quickly)

ETHEL
Dear Chelsea. I'm so glad you're home.

CHELSEA
Oh, God. I thought we'd never get here. We were rented a car that explodes every forty miles.

NORMAN
You rented a car?

CHELSEA
Yes, in Boston.

NORMAN
Huh. What sort of car is it?

CHELSEA
Oh, I don't know. Red, I think.

ETHEL
(Very cheerily)
Ooh! A red car!

NORMAN
No, I meant—what sort of make is it?

CHELSEA
(Stymied)
Um. I don't know.

ETHEL

She doesn't know, dear. It doesn't matter.

NORMAN

Of course it doesn't matter. I was just curious.

CHELSEA

Well, I should have looked, I guess. It's, um, very ugly and it breaks down a lot.

NORMAN

Ugly and it breaks down a lot. That sounds like a Nash. Probably your rent-a-car company bought up all the old Nashes all over the country and they're renting them to unsuspecting customers who can't differentiate between makes of automobile. That sounds like the sort of thing those people might do. You should go to Avis next time. They say they try harder, though it's probably not true.

CHELSEA

Well. Okay.
              (*She smiles at* ETHEL)
Well. The old house looks exactly the same.

NORMAN

The old house *is* exactly the same. Just older. Like its inhabitants.

ETHEL

(*Noticing something on a table, she steps to it quickly and brushes at it*)

And dustier. My goodness! I don't know where the dust comes from out here in the woods. The bugs bring it in, I think.

(*Another awkward moment*)

CHELSEA

Well . . .

ETHEL

Where is your friend? You did bring your friend, didn't you?

CHELSEA

I knew I was forgetting something.

NORMAN

It's still on then, huh?

CHELSEA

As far as I know. It was two minutes ago. I may have been deserted. It wouldn't be the first time. Are you two ready?

ETHEL

Of course. We can't wait.

NORMAN

That's right. We can't wait.

CHELSEA

Great.

(*She steps toward the door and calls*)

Hey! Come on in. Nobody's going to bite you. I hope.

(NORMAN *and* ETHEL *watch expectantly and*

**Scenes on the following pages
are from the ITC Films/IPC Films Production,
ON GOLDEN POND.**

Henry Fonda as Norman Thayer, and Katharine Hepburn
as Ethel Thayer, on the screen together for the first time.

Norman and Ethel arrive at their summer home on Golden Pond.

Grouchy Norman impatiently waits while Ethel greets Charlie, the mailman (William Lanteau).

Norman in front of the house.

Norman gets comfortable with a favorite book.

Ethel greets her daughter, Chelsea (Jane Fonda), and her boyfriend's son, Billy (Doug McKeon).

Ethel is amused as Norman plays parchesi with their daughter's dentist friend, Bill (Dabney Coleman).

Jane Fonda as Chelsea Thayer Wayne.

Norman has a serious conversion with Bill.

Ethel has a laugh with Charlie, the mailman.

Radiant Katharine Hepburn as Ethel Thayer.

Norman begins to enjoy the summer with Billy.

Ethel serves dinner to Norman and Billy.

Ethel and Norman listen to mating loons calling on the lake.

Ethel: "Chelsea, Norman is 80 years old. . . . When exactly do you expect this friendship to begin?"

Norman is pleased with his birthday cake.

After 48 years of marriage . . .

Norman clings to Billy after a boating accident.
Ethel speeds to the rescue with Charlie.

Norman: "Good God! Whatever have you got in here?"

Ethel: "Why don't they answer the phone?"

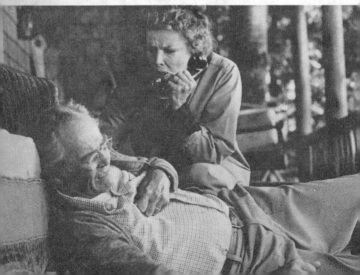

Frances Sternhagen and Tom Aldredge as Ethel and Norman in the original stage version of ON GOLDEN POND.

Ernest Thompson, author of ON GOLDEN POND.

BILLY RAY *enters. He is thirteen, short, flippant,*
but only to cover his awkwardness. He is eager and
bright. His hair is long, his posture terrible. He
carries a suitcase and stands at the doorway)

Mommy and Norman, this is Billy Ray.

(BILLY *sets down his suitcase and steps forward,*
putting out his hand. NORMAN *shakes it)*

BILLY

How ya doin'?

NORMAN

You seem awfully young to be a dentist.

BILLY

I'm a midget.

NORMAN

Oh, really?

CHELSEA
(Laughing)

This is Billy Ray, Junior.

NORMAN

Oh. I'm Norman Thayer, Junior.
               (To CHELSEA*)*
Where's . . . ?

CHELSEA

His dad is out trying to soothe the car.

ETHEL
(*Stepping forward and offering her hand*)
What a nice surprise! Hello, Billy. You can call me
Ethel. And you can call Norman Norman.
(BILLY *shakes her hand*)

CHELSEA
I like your logic, Mommy.
(*She steps to the door*)
I better see if Bill's gotten lost. He was trying to turn
around. He probably drove into the lake.
(*She exits.* ETHEL *steps to the door and looks out.*
NORMAN *and* BILLY *stare at each other*)

ETHEL
It's so dark outside. It never used to be this dark.

BILLY
I hear you turned eighty today.

NORMAN
Is that what you heard?

BILLY
Yes. That's really old.

NORMAN
Oh? You should meet my father.

BILLY
Your father's still alive?

NORMAN
No. But you should meet him.

ETHEL
(*Turning back to the room*)
This is so much fun! What a great surprise! Norman,
why don't we put Billy in Chelsea's old room and then
he can look out on the lake in the morning.

NORMAN
Why don't we put him out on the float, and he can
look at the lake all night long.

BILLY
I'd like that.

ETHEL
I'm afraid you'd be eaten alive by all the bugs.

NORMAN
So?

ETHEL
Norman, take him up and show him where everything is.

NORMAN
Come on, boy. Get your bag.
(BILLY *does, and he follows* NORMAN *up the stairs*)

BILLY
I just had a birthday, too. I turned thirteen two weeks
ago.

NORMAN
We're practically twins.

BILLY

We're sixty-seven years apart, and two weeks.

NORMAN

You're quick, aren't you?

BILLY

Oh, yes.
  (*They go into the room at the landing.* CHELSEA
  steps back in downstairs)

CHELSEA

He's coming. He thought he had to lock the doors.

ETHEL

Well, you never know, the changes around here.

CHELSEA
  (*Stepping to* ETHEL)
Norman looks very old.

ETHEL

Really? Well, I don't know.

CHELSEA

You look great, though.

ETHEL

Thank you. So do you. I love your hair like that.

CHELSEA
(*Surprised*)

You do?
(*She touches her hair quickly, then steps to her
mother.* NORMAN *appears on the landing to hear
the following*)

How's his mind? Is he remembering things any better?

ETHEL

Oh, he's all right.

NORMAN
(*Loudly*)

Come on, Billy, and I'll show you the bathroom, if I
can remember where it is.
(*He disappears into the hallway*)

CHELSEA

He really hasn't changed much, has he?

ETHEL

Nope, still impossible.
(*Quietly to* CHELSEA)

It means so much to him to have you here.

CHELSEA

Yeah. Great. Now he's got somebody to pick on.

ETHEL

Oh, stop. Thank you for coming.

CHELSEA

Thank you for inviting me. Your letter made it sound like he was ready for the home.

ETHEL

Well, I was very concerned. I still am. You never know about these things.

(*A brief pause. They smile at each other tentatively*)

CHELSEA

Well, it's nice to be here.

(BILL RAY *appears at the door. He is attractive and well-dressed, a ready smile. He tends to be serious, but he has a good sense of humor when he remembers to use it. He works at being an intellectual, and is a bit cautious in life. He has extra personality supplies, on reserve, just below the surface. He carries several packages and a suitcase. He is out of breath. He sets his load by the door*)

Look at you. You made it.

BILL

Yes. I think I saw a bear.

CHELSEA

I doubt that. Bill, this is my mother. Mommy, Bill Ray.

ETHEL

(*Shaking* BILL's *hand*)

I'm very pleased you could come. Welcome to Golden Pond.

BILL

Thank you. Do you have a dog?

ETHEL

What? No.

(*To* CHELSEA)

You know, I tried to interest Norman in getting a dog this summer, but he went into some morbid diatribe about how unfair it is to take on a puppy if you're planning to die soon.

CHELSEA

You could have gotten him an old dog. Something on its last leg.

ETHEL

Well, Norman is still in mourning for Chum, I'm afraid.

CHELSEA

(*To* BILL)

Chum was a Labrador retriever who passed on just twenty short years ago.

BILL

(*Not exactly following*)

Oh. Do any of your neighbors have dogs?

ETHEL

Um. No, I don't believe so.

BILL

Then I definitely saw a bear.

ETHEL

Oh, no, I don't think there'd be a bear out there this time of year. They go pretty far into the woods when the summer people show up. There's a lot of very nasty moths flying around, though, I'm sorry to say.

BILL

This was kind of big for a moth.

CHELSEA

Probably a wild boar, then. Bill, you want to visit the men's room before you go through the shock of meeting my father?

BILL

Huh? Uh. No. I'm all right.
(*There is a clatter on the stairs, and* BILLY *leaps down, followed by* NORMAN)

CHELSEA

Too late anyway.

BILLY

Dad. They *do* have indoor plumbing.

BILL
(*Embarrassed*)

Oh. Good.

BILLY
(*Crossing down into the room*)
Chelsea was bullshitting us.
(NORMAN *loves this*)

BILL

Billy.

CHELSEA
(To ETHEL)
I always try to paint a rustic picture of life on Golden Pond.

ETHEL

Oh, it's rustic all right.

BILL

It's lovely, though. Lovely rusticity.
(NORMAN *has arrived in the center of the room.*
BILL *turns to him*)
Hi.

NORMAN

We've been peeing indoors for forty years.

BILL

Oh. You must be Norman.

NORMAN

Yes, I must be. Who are you?

BILL

Bill Ray.
(*He puts out his hand.* NORMAN *shakes it*)

NORMAN

Bill Ray. The dentist?

BILL

Uh. Yes.

NORMAN

Want to see my teeth?

(*He bares them*)

ETHEL

Norman.

BILL

(*Smiling*)

I just want to tell you how glad I am to be here, sir. Chelsea talks so much about you and your wife and your wonderful house on the lake, and I'm very pleased that she's brought us here.

NORMAN

(*He stares at* BILL *a moment, then turns to* CHELSEA)

Charlie's been asking for you.

CHELSEA

Charlie?

(NORMAN *responds by mimicking* CHARLIE's *laugh*)

Holy Mackinoly.

(*To* BILL)

Charlie is our mailman. He was also my boyfriend every summer for twelve years. He taught me everything.

BILL

(*Goodnaturedly*)

Isn't that amazing?

NORMAN
It is when you know Charlie.
(*A pause*)

CHELSEA
Well. I'm going to say hello to the lake. Anyone like to come?

BILLY
Me. I've never seen anyone say hello to a lake.

CHELSEA
Then this will be a valuable experience for you, wise guy. It's always my first order of business when I get to Golden Pond. Coming, Mommy?

ETHEL
Yes! Want to take the boat?

BILLY
Yeah!

CHELSEA
Why not? Let's go, Bill.

BILL
Where? Outside?

CHELSEA
That's where the lake is.
(*She heads for the door.* ETHEL *and* BILLY *follow*)
Coming, Norman?

NORMAN

Nope.

ETHEL

Oh, come on.

NORMAN

No. I'm just going to sit here and enjoy the quiet.

CHELSEA

Oh. Um . . .
(*She looks at* ETHEL, *then at* BILL)

BILL

I think I'll stay, too.

ETHEL

Come on, Norman.

NORMAN

Don't be silly. I want to sit here and enjoy the quiet.
With Bill. We can talk baseball.

BILL

Great.

CHELSEA

Great.

ETHEL

I'll get the yard light switch.
(*She reaches by the door and flicks it. The trees
light up*)

I generally keep it off to discourage the June bugs.
>   (*She starts to open the door*)
Now, we're going to have to make a run for it all at
once. Ready?
>   (*She opens the door and pushes* BILLY *through.*
>   CHELSEA *follows*)

CHELSEA

The screen door has fallen down. ·

ETHEL

Oh, really? Norman will fix it.
>   (*She steps through the door, closing it. Their voices
>   can be heard as they cross the porch and disappear
>   down the steps.* NORMAN, *in the meantime, has sat
>   down in his chair.* BILL *stands for a moment, a
>   shade uncomfortable*)

BILL

So. You're a baseball fan, huh?

NORMAN

No.

BILL

Oh.
>   (*They look at each other a moment*)
I like baseball. I like the Dodgers.

NORMAN

Oh, really? They moved out west somewhere, didn't
they?

BILL

Um. Yes. To Los Angeles. Some years ago.

NORMAN

They still in the big leagues?

BILL

Oh, yes. They're a real powerhouse in the National
League West.

NORMAN

Well, bless their little hearts.
            (*There is another long pause*)

BILL

Um. How does it feel to turn eighty?

NORMAN

It feels twice as bad as it did turning forty.

BILL

Oh, well, I know what that's like.

NORMAN

Do you?

BILL

Yes. I turned forty five years ago. I'm forty-five now.
            (NORMAN *nods*)
I . . . love your house.

NORMAN

Thank you. It's not for sale.

BILL

Oh, no, I wasn't thinking about buying it. I just like it.

NORMAN

Oh. Me, too.

BILL

It has a charming ambience.

NORMAN

Does it?

BILL

Oh, yes. Norman?

NORMAN

Yes?

BILL

May I call you Norman?

NORMAN

I believe you just did.

BILL

I don't want to press.

NORMAN

No.

BILL

I'll call you Norman then.

NORMAN

Fine.

BILL

What shall I call your wife?

NORMAN

How about Ethel? That's her name. Ethel Thayer. Thoundth like I'm lithping, doethn't it? Ethel Thayer. It almost kept her from marrying me. She wanted me to change my last name to hers.

BILL

What was that?

NORMAN

I don't remember. Ethel's all you need to know. That's the name she goes by.

BILL

I never knew. Chelsea always calls her Mommy.

NORMAN

There's a reason for that.

BILL

But she calls you Norman.

NORMAN

There's a reason for that, too.
(He pauses)
I *am* her father, if you're trying to figure it out. I'm her father but not her daddy. Ethel is her mommy, and I'm Norman.

BILL
(*Confused*)
Oh. Is it all right if I sit down?

NORMAN
As far as I'm concerned it is.
 (BILL *sits.* NORMAN *stares at him.* BILL *tries to smile*)
There's something I want to ask you.

BILL
(*Nervously*)
Yes?

NORMAN
What sort of car did you rent to drive up here?

BILL
Oh. Um. Pontiac. Firebird.

NORMAN
Oh?

BILL
Yes. It's um, it's a good car.

NORMAN
I wouldn't know. What kind of car do you have where you live, out there in Disneyland?

BILL
Um, Mercedes, 480 SL. It's um, it's a good car.

NORMAN
German, isn't it?

BILL

Yes.

(NORMAN *considers this, he nods, then abruptly rises*)

NORMAN

I think I'll start a new book. See if I can finish it before I'm finished myself. Maybe a novelette.

(*He steps to the shelves and studies the collection*)

Maybe something in a Reader's Digest Abridged.

(*He pulls down a book*)

Here's *Swiss Family Robinson*. Ever read it?

BILL

Oh, yes. It's great. I'd recommend it.

NORMAN

No need for that. I've read it, too.

(*He sits again*)

But my mind's going so it'll all be new to me.

(*He opens the book*)

Has that son of yours read this book?

BILL

I . . . don't think so.

NORMAN

Your son hasn't read *Swiss Family Robinson*?

BILL

No. But I intend to have him read it. I'm afraid his mother's been the motivating force in his life the last few years, the poor kid, and now I'm making a move to eradicate some of the . . . dishevelment.

(NORMAN *stares at* BILL *without comment. He returns to his book.* BILL *feels compelled to communicate*)

Yeah, things are coming together for me pretty nicely now. The practice is real strong, and I'm feeling very good about myself. Meeting Chelsea has been a major . . . thing. And she's really flowering. She likes her job a lot, and she's been doing some beautiful paintings. We have a very kinetic relationship. Very positive. I'm sure you'd be pleased.

(NORMAN *looks up. There is a pause.* BILL *smiles*)

NORMAN

What do you charge for a filling?

BILL

Huh?

NORMAN

You're a dentist, aren't you? What do you charge for a filling?

BILL

Um. Forty dollars, generally.

NORMAN

Forty dollars?! Good God! My brother charged five dollars for a filling right up until 1973 when he raised it to seven. That's when I stopped going to him.

BILL

Your brother is a dentist?

NORMAN

He was. When he was living.

BILL

Isn't that amazing?

NORMAN

I don't know. I think every family has one.
(*He returns to his book.* BILL *studies him, then chooses his words with care*)

BILL

Um. Norman. Um. I don't want to offend you, but there's a rather important little topic that I feel I have to broach.

NORMAN
(*Looking up*)

I beg your pardon?

BILL

I don't want to offend you, but . . . if it's all right with you, we'd like to sleep together.

NORMAN

What do you mean?

BILL

We'd like to sleep . . . together . . . in the same room . . . in the same bed. If you don't find that offensive.

NORMAN

All three of you?

BILL

What? Oh, no. Just two.

NORMAN

You and Billy?

BILL

No.

NORMAN

Not Chelsea and Billy?

BILL

No.

NORMAN
(*Pausing*)

That leaves only Chelsea and you then.

BILL

Yes.

NORMAN

Why would I find that offensive? You're not planning on doing something unusual, are you?

BILL

Oh, no. Just . . . .
(*He can't go on*)

NORMAN

That doesn't seem too offensive, as long as you're quiet.

BILL

Great.

NORMAN

Chelsea always used to sleep in the same bed with her husband.

BILL

Oh, I'm sure.

NORMAN

And Ethel and I do, you know. We sleep together. Been doing it for years.

BILL

Well, of course. But you're married and all.

NORMAN

So?

BILL

Well . . .

NORMAN

I think I'm beginning to see this more clearly. It's a moral issue, isn't it?

BILL

Well, it's just that we're of different generations, different mores. . . .

NORMAN

What is a more? I've never known.

BILL

Um . . . a custom, I'd say. Or something.

NORMAN

Go on. I shouldn't have interrupted.

BILL

Well, it's just a matter of points of view. . . .

NORMAN
(Interrupting)
Forgive me for interrupting.

BILL

Oh. Of course.
(Starting again)
It's just that I don't want our relationship to . . .

NORMAN

It's a terrible social problem, I think.

BILL

Um . . . ?

NORMAN

Interrupting. Not listening. The art of conversation
went out with radio probably.

BILL

Yes.

NORMAN

Or maybe with mirrors.

BILL

Um . . .

NORMAN

Ever notice how people start to check themselves out in a mirror or a window or your eyeglasses when they're supposed to be listening?

BILL

Yes, I have noticed that.

NORMAN

It's a shifty sort of quality, I think.

BILL

Yes.

NORMAN

Or perhaps it's just a form of egocentricity.

BILL

Yeah.

NORMAN

I do it.

BILL

You do?

NORMAN

Sure. Conversations bore me to tears. I always look for a little divertissement while I'm waiting for my turn to talk.

BILL

Huh.

NORMAN

Pretty shabby, huh?

BILL

Well . . .

NORMAN

I don't do it with Ethel. She's so pretty, isn't she?

BILL

Yes.

NORMAN

After all these years I still can't get over how pretty she is. Or how handsome I am. That's the real reason I always look for a mirror. I like to keep checking. Make sure I haven't faded.

BILL

Oh.

NORMAN

They say you fade with old age. They say your looks just go. I haven't seen a sign of it.

BILL

No, indeed.

NORMAN

What were we talking about?

BILL

Um . . .

NORMAN

Sex, I believe. You were concerned that my morals somehow wouldn't gel with yours.

BILL

Yes.

NORMAN

Don't be silly. I'd be delighted to have you abusing my daughter under my own roof.

BILL

Norman . . .

NORMAN

Would you like the room where I first violated her mother, or would you be interested in the master bedroom?

BILL

Um . . .

NORMAN

Ethel and your son and I could all sleep out back and you could do it right there on the hearth. Like that idea?

BILL

(*He's embarrassed, but he's also heard enough. He smiles at* NORMAN *and shakes his head*)
You're having a good time, aren't you?

NORMAN

Hmmm?

BILL

Chelsea told me all about you, about how you like to have a good old time with people's heads. She does it, too, sometimes, and sometimes I can get into it. Sometimes not. I just want you to know that I'm very good at recognizing *crap* when I hear it. You know, it's not imperative that you and I be friends, but it might be *nice*. I'm sure you're a fascinating person, and I'm sure it would be fascinating to get to know you. That's obviously not an easy task. But it's all right, you go ahead and be as *poopy* as you want, to quote Chelsea, and I'll be as receptive and as pleasant as I can. I just want you to bear in mind while we're sitting here smiling at each other and you're jerking me around and I'm feeling like a real asshole that I know precisely what you're up to and that I can take only so much of it. Okay? Good.

(*He pauses. Waits for a reaction.* NORMAN *has been listening very intently*)

Now. Having said all that, and noticing that you haven't shot me yet, uh, let's get back to the issue at hand. What's the bottom line on the illicit sex question?

NORMAN

(*He stares at* BILL *for a long moment, then smiles*)

Very nice. Good speech! I liked that a lot. Real spunk! Mmm. Yes. Very good! So, bottom line, huh? You're a bottom-line man. All right. Here's the bottom line: oh-kay.

BILL

Um . . . ?

NORMAN

Ethel and I haven't always been married. It just seems that way. We tipped over a canoe or two in our day, trying to accommodate another generation's *mores*.
(*He pauses*)
You seem like a nice person, a bit verbose perhaps, a bit outspoken, but . . . nice.

BILL

Thank you.

NORMAN

And you're right about me. I *am* fascinating.

BILL

I'm sure you are.

NORMAN

Here now, what exactly goes on in a kinetic relationship, other than what we've just discussed?

BILL

Oh, the usual. We play a lot of tennis, we go out dancing. That sort of thing.

NORMAN

Does Chelsea like dancing?

BILL

Yes. She seems to. We both enjoy . . . tripping the light fantastic.

NORMAN

Do you? I've never taken Ethel dancing. I've always felt badly about that. I'm sure she would have liked it. She's the type, you know.

BILL
(Brightly)

Well. It's not too late.

NORMAN

That's what you think. My mind and my body are having a great race to see who can poop out first. I'd put my money on the body, but you never know.

BILL

Well, you certainly seem to enjoy your life now anyway.

NORMAN

Do I?

BILL

You seem to. You should.

NORMAN
(Thinking about it)

I suppose I do.
(A beat)
I didn't mean to weight down our conversation. We can go back to talking about sex if you like.

BILL

Oh, no. That's okay.

NORMAN

I like talking about sex. Anything you want to know just ask me.

BILL

Okay. I . . . I do want to make sure I have this little matter clear in my mind. Chelsea and I *can* sleep together, right?

NORMAN

Yes! Please do! Just don't let Ethel catch you.
(*There is the sound of footsteps on the porch steps, and then* BILLY *comes bounding in the upstage door*)

BILLY

Dad! I paddled a canoe! It's a boat, just like the Indians had!
(BILL *stands*)

NORMAN

Actually the Indians used a different grade of aluminum.

BILLY

Chelsea wants you to come down, Dad. She and Ethel are going skinny-dipping.

BILL

Skinny-dipping?
(*He barely dares look at* NORMAN)
Um . . .

NORMAN

Go ahead. Permissiveness runs rampant up here on Golden Pond.

(BILL *walks slowly to the front door. He turns.*)

BILL

Are there ever any bears around these parts?

NORMAN

Sure. Black bears and grizzlies. One came along here last month and ate an old lesbian.

BILL

Uh . . .

BILLY

Go on, Dad. He's bullshitting you.

BILL

Heh.

(*He still isn't sure. He stares out the window, looks back to* NORMAN. *To the window, to* NORMAN.)

God, I hope I live through the next few days.

(*He exits.* BILLY *steps down to* NORMAN)

NORMAN

You like that word, don't you? Bullshit.

BILLY

Yeah.

NORMAN

It's a good word.

BILLY
You going skinny-dipping?

NORMAN
Nope. You?

BILLY
Naw. I try to be selective about who I flash in front of.

NORMAN
(*Not following*)
Oh?

BILLY
That canoe is really bitchin'.

NORMAN
(*Not sure*)
Bitchin'?

BILLY
Yeah. Chelsea says you're a real heavy-duty fisher-man. She calls you the old man of the sea.

NORMAN
Ah. I've caught a few. You fish?

BILLY
No.

NORMAN
Want to go sometime?

BILLY

Definitely.

NORMAN

All right. We'll see. What do you think of your father?

BILLY

To tell you the truth—he's not bad.

NORMAN

He seems like a nice person.
   (*They stare at each other a moment.* BILLY *wanders across the stage*)
Why do you walk with your shoulders all bent like that?

BILLY

I have a lot on my mind.

NORMAN

Oh.
          (*He studies* BILLY *for a moment*)
Well, what do you do out there in California, since you don't fish? I mean, what does one do for recreation, when one is thirteen and not in school?

BILLY

Cruise chicks.

NORMAN

Um . . . ?

BILLY

Meet 'em. Girls. Try to pick them up.

NORMAN

Oh. And what do you do with them when you have
them?

BILLY

Suck face.

NORMAN

I beg your pardon?

BILLY
(*Explaining*)
You know. Kiss. Suck face—kiss.

NORMAN

Oh. Oh . . . oh.
(*He stares at* BILLY, *then looks at the book he still
holds*)
Ever read this book? *Swiss Family Robinson*?

BILLY

No.

NORMAN

Go read it.

BILLY

Now?

NORMAN

Yes. Go upstairs and read the first chapter. And give
me a report tomorrow.
(*He hands* BILLY *the book*)
Go on.

BILLY

Well, I thought we were going to have a party.

NORMAN

I'll call you when the party's underway, if it ever is. Go on. Go read the first chapter. You'll like it.
(BILLY *obeys. There's something in* NORMAN's *authority that* BILLY *responds to, not unfavorably. He marches up the stairs*)
Let me see you stand up straight.
(BILLY *stops and scowls at* NORMAN)
Come on. Nobody has that much on his mind.
(BILLY *straightens*)
Ah! Very good! You should try that more often. It will make it easier to bear your heavy load.

BILLY

Yeah, well this is kind of a tricky time in my life. I'll pass through it.
(*Remembering his manners*)
Um. I'm glad I got to come here. It's nowhere near as weird as Chelsea said it was. And neither are you.

NORMAN

Thank you.
(BILLY *exits.* ETHEL *comes bursting in the upstage door, fully dressed, and swatting at the moths*)
I thought you'd be nude.

ETHEL

Sorry. The water feels lovely, but I didn't want to overwhelm Chelsea's friend on his first night here.
(*She comes down into the room*)
Have you been picking on him?.

NORMAN

Yes. He found me fascinating.

ETHEL

He's very sweet, isn't he?

NORMAN

I don't know.

ETHEL

Chelsea says he's very funny.

NORMAN

He is. He's a scream.

ETHEL

She really likes him, I can tell that. Says he's very smart.

NORMAN

And rich. She tell you that? Forty dollars a filling.

ETHEL

Forty dollars?!

NORMAN

That's enough to keep you off sweets, isn't it?

ETHEL

Well, he'd be quite a catch, wouldn't he?

NORMAN

He said they want to sleep together.

ETHEL

I expected that. Well. Why not? They're big people.

NORMAN

Yes.

ETHEL

You and I did it. Didn't we?

NORMAN

Yes, I told him that.

ETHEL
(*Blushes*)

Well, you didn't have to tell him. I think I better get us some dinner together. You must be starved half to death.

NORMAN

And then some.

ETHEL
(*Heading for the kitchen*)

Where's the boy?

NORMAN

I sent him to his room with a good book.

ETHEL

Oh.
          (*She looks up toward the landing*)
Well.
     (*She starts into the kitchen, stops, comes back to*
     NORMAN)
Norman.

NORMAN

Yes.

ETHEL

Norman. Chelsea wants us to do something. For her.

NORMAN

What?

ETHEL

She wants to leave Billy here with us for a month.

NORMAN

Which Billy?

ETHEL

The little one. *Billy.* Bill is supposed to have him for the summer, and he'd be miserable in Europe. They could pick him up in August. And they could be alone. Bill seems very nice, and Chelsea needs someone nice. Couldn't we do that for her?

NORMAN

What would we do with the boy? What would I say to him?

ETHEL

You'd think of something. Norman, let's do it. Let's say we'll do it, and give Chelsea some happiness. Yes?

NORMAN
(*After the briefest pause*)

All right.

ETHEL
(*Hugging him*)

You poop. I love you. We're going to have a splendid time, the three of us. Aren't we?

NORMAN

I don't know. We might.

ETHEL

You really are the sweetest man in the world. And I'm the only one who knows. I've *got* to make some dinner.
(*She heads for the kitchen*)
Can you hold out ten more minutes?

NORMAN

No. I'm going to bed.

ETHEL
(*Stopping*)

Oh. You're not.

NORMAN

No, I'm not. I was just bullshitting you.
(*She shakes her head*)

CURTAIN

ACT TWO

Scene One

The middle of August. Early morning.

The room is the same, minus the party decorations. Two new photos are on the mantel, and several postcards. Outside, the sky is gray.

After a moment, the kitchen door opens and NOR-MAN tiptoes in. He is wearing old, old pants and a fisherman's vest, and one of the floppy hats. He stands at the bottom of the stairs and calls, softly.

NORMAN
Are you up? Let's go. Don't wake up the old lady. *(He crosses back to the rack and picks up two fishing poles, then gently opens the front door. He is moving much faster than we've seen him. He pushes open the screen door, which is, remarkably enough, fastened on. He closes it carefully and disappears down the porch steps. No sooner has he gone than the downstage door opens and BILLY enters, wearing shorts and a t-shirt, and another one of NORMAN's hats. His posture has improved. He carries a bait bucket, which he sets on the platform. He exits into the kitchen. As the door closes, ETHEL appears on the stairs. She wears a robe. She*

walks down to the platform, her attention focused on a beam above her. She makes a face at it, and then crosses purposefully to the downstage door and exits. NORMAN *enters upstage. He sees the bait bucket and stares at it, puzzled. He picks it up, and steps up to the landing. He knocks on the door)*

Let's go, boy. I've got the bait bucket. Don't wake up Ethel!

(He steps back down and exits into the room stage right. BILLY *comes out of the kitchen, carrying a tall pile of cookies in both hands. He arrives at a pack hanging from the hat rack, but he can't maneuver the cookies and the bag both. He steps to the couch and attempts to balance the cookies on the back of it. They fall behind the couch)*

BILLY
(Quietly. Sounding like NORMAN*)*

Good God!

(He grabs the bag and kneels quickly behind the couch, out of sight. ETHEL *enters downstage, carrying a long leaf rake. She stands beneath the beam and stares up at it. She raises the rake high over her head and concentrates on the beam.* NORMAN *enters, laden down with a fish net, several boat cushions, a tackle box, an umbrella, a coil of rope, and the bait bucket. He doesn't see* ETHEL, *his vision being limited by his load.* BILLY *is still hidden behind the couch.* NORMAN *goes to the foot of the stairs and calls softly)*

NORMAN

Let's go, let's go, let's go!

(*He stares up at the closed door, annoyed.* ETHEL *hasn't particularly noticed him, her concentration on the beam being so intense. Now she's found her foe and she swings her rake mightily. It misses the beam altogether, and smacks down on the floor beside* NORMAN. *He is more than a little surprised. He drops his collection.* BILLY's *head pops up; he looks, then goes back out of sight*)

Good God! You must be mad! You're trying to kill me!

(*He's not bothering with quiet now*)

ETHEL

That's not true. I was trying to kill a daddy-long-legs, but he got away.

NORMAN

You shouldn't be allowed to carry a dangerous weapon like that.

ETHEL
(*Looking up*)

I see him now. Way up there. Laughing at me.

NORMAN

Daddy-long-legs don't laugh.

ETHEL

There's no need for you to go on shouting. You'll wake the boy.

NORMAN
(*Shouting*)

Good! I've been trying to wake him for twenty minutes. We're going fishing.

ETHEL

Oh, let him sleep. You drag him out every day, poor thing. We have enough fish now, as it is. What are we going to do with them all?

NORMAN

Feed them to the daddy-long-legs.
(*He calls*)
You! Billy! Get it in gear, boy!
(*To* ETHEL)
Know what that means?

ETHEL

Yes. It means that you've lost the last of your marbles. Let him sleep. It's going to rain anyway. The loons were calling for it all night long.

NORMAN

I didn't hear them.

ETHEL

You weren't up hunting daddy-long-legs. Back and forth they went. "Rain, rain. Send us the rain."

NORMAN

I don't believe they actually said, "Rain, rain, send us the rain."

ETHEL

Well, they said it in loon language.

NORMAN

I wasn't aware that you were skilled in translating loon language.

ETHEL

Well, I am.
(*Suddenly there comes the sound of a loon calling.* NORMAN *and* ETHEL *look at each other*)

NORMAN

Well? What's the weather forecast now?

ETHEL

Still rain.
(*The call is repeated*)
Isn't it lovely? What a sweet song they sing.
(*Again the call*)
They must be right out in front.

NORMAN

Sounds to me like they're right behind the couch. Out, boy!
(BILLY *rises from behind the couch, grinning from ear to ear. He calls again*)

ETHEL

Oh, we have a joker here.

BILLY

Good morning, loonies.

ETHEL

Oh, yes, very funny.

BILLY

Let's get it in gear, Norman.

NORMAN

Watch it.

(ETHEL *watches as* BILLY *comes around with his
bag of cookies. He bends to pick up some of what*
NORMAN *has dropped.* NORMAN *shrugs and joins
him.* ETHEL *smiles and shakes her head*)

ETHEL

You two will be sorry when it begins to pour.

NORMAN

It's a chance we have to take. Billy still has to catch,
one more biggie. It's starting to depress him that I've
outbiggied him.

BILLY

Today's the day. I can feel it.

ETHEL

What's in the bag, Billy?

BILLY

This bag? Food. Good food.

ETHEL

Not my tollhouse cookies by any chance?

BILLY

Uh. Some.

ETHEL
(*Stepping to him*)

Hand it over.
(*He does, reluctantly.* ETHEL *takes the bag into the
kitchen*)

NORMAN

Spoilsport.
(*To* BILLY)

Oh, well. We can always eat raw fish like the orientals
do.

BILLY

Blecch.

NORMAN

Of course you may never get any taller. Got a book
with you?

BILLY

Yes.
(*He doesn't, but he crosses quickly to the shelves
and pulls down a book*)
A Connecticut Yankee in King Arthur's Court.

NORMAN

Ah.
(ETHEL *returns with a different bag, a larger one
and full. She hangs it around* BILLY's *neck*)

ETHEL

You'll find a few cookies in there, and some biscuits, along with two tuna-fish sandwiches each, a thermos of milk, and a nice jar of fresh raspberries, just picked.

NORMAN

When in the name of God did you have time to do all that?

ETHEL

Between skirmishes in the daddy-long-legs war.

NORMAN

Oh. Didn't have any fall in the tuna fish, did you?

ETHEL

No.

(*As* NORMAN *piles on the last of the gear*)

BILLY

Smooth move, Norman.

NORMAN

Thanks, cool breeze, That's jive talk, Ethel.

ETHEL

That's nice.

(*The boys head for the upstage door*)

NORMAN

Goodbye, woman. Hold it! Where's my chair? I can't fish without my chair.

BILLY

It's in the back by the picnic table.

NORMAN

What's it doing there?

BILLY

You were sitting on it yesterday while you watched me clean the fish.

NORMAN

Ohhh.

ETHEL

Tsk. Has he been making you clean those stupid fish?

BILLY

Yeah.

NORMAN

That's right, Ethel. He cleans the stupid ones and I clean the smart ones. Fortunately the smart ones are too smart to get caught. That's why they're in schools, ha ha!

ETHEL

Oh, Lord.

BILLY
(*To* NORMAN)
You're really becoming a nitwit, aren't you?

NORMAN

A *nitwit*? Hear that, Ethel? This poor child is starting to talk like an old lady. Get my chair, boy!

ETHEL

Norman, his hands are full.

BILLY

That's right, my hands are full.

NORMAN

So? You've got teeth, don't you?

ETHEL

Norman, *get* the chair.

NORMAN

Good God!

ETHEL

Poor Billy ends up doing all your chores.

NORMAN

What's the point of having a dwarf if he doesn't do chores?

(*He kisses* ETHEL *with great flair, and exits. She closes the door and turns to find* BILLY *smiling at her. She helps him with the gear*)

ETHEL

Here, we'll have to start all over.

BILLY

Don't you get lonely here all by yourself?

ETHEL

Nope. Not too much.

BILLY

You could come with us, you know.

ETHEL

No, thank you, I've never liked fishing. I used to go
with my father and brother, but I didn't like it. It
always seemed like the dead fish were staring at me.

BILLY

I know what you mean. But I like fishing.

ETHEL

I'm awfully glad. I know Norman loves having you
go.

BILLY

Oh, yeah, we have a lot of fun. We don't just fish, you
know.

ETHEL

No?

BILLY

Nope. We make good use of our time. Norman makes
me practice my French, and I make him tell me
stories from the old days. You and Norman must have
had a pretty nifty time way back then. I was surprised.

ETHEL

Uh-huh.

BILLY

It's good for his mind, you know, to dig back like that.
Sometimes he calls me Chelsea.

ETHEL

Oh Well, you probably remind him of her in some
ways.

BILLY

Yeah. I always say, "Norman, you know I'm not
Chelsea, I'm Billy." He's okay. I keep after him.

ETHEL

Good.

BILLY

What do you do while we're out there?

ETHEL

Oh. I make good use of my time, too. Today I'm
going to go through this whole box of our old pictures
and sort out the ones we don't need anymore, and
try to throw them away, and probably end up putting
them right back in the box like I do every year. And
then I'll take a walk over to Spruce Cove, if it clears,
and look for the loons. And I'll ride my bike, take a
swim maybe, things like that.

BILLY
(Approving)
That sounds pretty exciting.

NORMAN
(Offstage)

Hey! Allons! Début!

BILLY
(Calling)

Je viens!

(To Ethel)

That means I'm coming.

ETHEL

I'll get la porte.

BILLY

I wouldn't worry about Norman. I'll keep an eye on him.

ETHEL
(She kisses him)

Thanks, dear.

BILLY

Goodbye, woman!
(He exits. She watches him go, closes the screen door. She turns back to the room, stops for a beat, then walks to her cardboard box. She opens it and peers inside, but her attention is caught by a daddy-long-legs on the mantel. She grabs a newspaper and pursues the bug)

ETHEL

All right, hold it right there! Stay still! What's the matter with you? Look out, Elmer, he's right behind you! Oh, fiddle. Go on, climb the chimney, I don't care. Tsk. Are you laughing at me?
(She takes down Elmer and hugs him to her)

Oh, Elmer, isn't he awful? Elmer, Elmer, Elmer.
> (*She stands for a moment, lost in thought. The
> sound of the motorboat interrupts her. She turns
> and walks to the window. She waves. She takes
> Elmer's hand and waves it. She sits on the steps*)

They say the lake is dying, but I don't believe it. They
say all those houses along Koochakiyi Shores are kill-
ing Golden Pond. See, Elmer, no more yellow tents in
the trees, no more bell calling the girls to supper. I
left you in this window, Elmer, sitting on the sill, so
you could look out at Camp Koochakiyi, when I was
eight and nine and ten. And I'd stand on the bank,
across the cove, at sunset, and I'd wave. And you always waved back, didn't you, Elmer?
> (*She thinks for a moment, and then sings softly*)

I can see the stars
Way up in the sky,
> From my tent on the bank of the lake
> At Camp Koochakiyi.
> Camp Koochakiyi.
>> (*She stops and considers it*)

What a terrible song.
>> (*But she sings on*)

I can see the . . . trees
And the . . . hills beyond,
From my tent on the bank of the lake
Called Golden Pond,
On Golden Pond.
>> (*She stands and begins her camp dance*)

We are the girls from Camp Koochakiyi.
You can tell who we are by the gleam
In our eyes.
>> (*The dance becomes more elaborate*)

Our minds are clear and our hearts
Are strong.
We are dancing here, but we won't be long.
There will soon be deer where there now
Are fawns.
But we'll remember our years on Golden Pond.
  On Golden Pond.

> (*Near the end of this performance the downstage
> door opens and* CHELSEA *enters on tiptoe. She
> freezes when she sees her mother. More than em-
> barrassed, she watches with almost sadness in her
> eyes.* ETHEL *senses* CHELSEA's *presence and stops
> dancing, mortified. They stare at each other for a
> moment.* CHELSEA *raises her hand in an Indian
> salute*)

CHELSEA

How.

ETHEL

How'd you get here?

CHELSEA

I rented a car. A Volare. It's made by Plymouth. I got
it from Avis.

> (*She walks to* ETHEL *They embrace*)

They *do* try hard.

ETHEL

You're not supposed to come till the fifteenth.

CHELSEA

Today's the fifteenth.

ETHEL

No!

CHELSEA

'Fraid so.

ETHEL

Well. No wonder you're here.

CHELSEA

Still have the kid or did you drown him?

ETHEL

Still have him.

CHELSEA

Are he and Norman asleep?

ETHEL

You must be joking. They're out on the lake already, antagonizing the fish. Still have Bill or did you drown him?

CHELSEA

Still got him. But he's not with me. He went back to the coast. He had a mouth that needed looking into.

ETHEL

Oh. You must have left Boston at the crack of dawn.

CHELSEA

I left Boston in the middle of the night. I felt like driving. I didn't feel like getting lost, but it worked out that way.

ETHEL

If you'd come more often, you wouldn't get lost.

CHELSEA

You're right. If I promise to come more often will you give me a cup of coffee?

ETHEL

All right. I could do that. Yes. You must have had a lovely time in Europe. You look wonderful.
(*She exits into the kitchen*)

CHELSEA

I do? I did. I had a lovely time.
(*Peers out at the lake*)

ETHEL
(*Offstage*)

I always thought Norman and I should travel, but we never got to it somehow. I'm not sure Norman would like Europe.

CHELSEA

He wouldn't like Italy.

ETHEL
(*Offstage*)

No?

CHELSEA

Too many Italians.

ETHEL
(*Enters*)

I've got the perker going. See the boys?

CHELSEA

Yes. What are they doing out there? It's starting to rain.

ETHEL

Ah, well. I told Norman not to go. The loons have been calling for it. I'm afraid Norman doesn't give them much credence.

CHELSEA

They're going to get drenched.

ETHEL

I think between the two of them they have sense enough to come in out of the rain. At least I hope they do.
(*A moment passes as they look out at the lake*)
Isn't it beautiful?

CHELSEA
(*She nods and looks at* ETHEL)

Look at you. You've had that robe for as long as I can remember.

ETHEL
(*She tries to arrange it*)

It looks like it, doesn't it?

CHELSEA

It looks great.
> (*She stares at* ETHEL, *moved. She steps to her and hugs her emphatically*)

ETHEL

You're in a huggy mood today. What's the matter?

CHELSEA

You seem different.

ETHEL

You mean old.

CHELSEA

I don't know.

ETHEL

Well, that's what happens if you live long enough. You end up being old. It's one of the disadvantages of a long life. I still prefer it to the alternative.

CHELSEA

How does it really make you feel?

ETHEL

Not much different. A little more aware of the sunrises, I guess. And the sunsets.

CHELSEA

It makes *me* mad.

ETHEL

Ah, well, it doesn't exactly make me want to jump up
and down.
(CHELSEA *hugs* ETHEL *again*)
Oh, dear. They're not digging the grave yet. Come sit
down. You must be exhausted.
(ETHEL *sits.* CHELSEA *wanders*)

CHELSEA

Have Billy and Norman gotten along all right?

ETHEL

Billy is the happiest thing that's happened to Norman
since Roosevelt. I should have rented him a thirteen-
year-old boy years ago.

CHELSEA

You could have traded me in.
(ETHEL *laughs*)
Billy reminds me of myself out there, way back when.
Except I think he makes a better son than I did.

ETHEL

Well, you made a very nice daughter.

CHELSEA

Does Billy put the worm on the hook by himself?

ETHEL

I'm really not sure.

CHELSEA

I hope so. You lose points if you throw up, I remember that. I always apologized to those nice worms before I impaled them. Well, they'll get even with me some day, won't they?

ETHEL

You're beginning to sound an awful lot like your father.

CHELSEA

Uh oh.
(*Changing direction*)
Thank you for taking care of Billy.

ETHEL

Thank *you*. I'm glad it gives us another chance to see you. Plus, it's been a tremendous education. Norman's vocabulary will never be the same but that's all right.

CHELSEA
(*Turning to the mantel and picking up a picture*)
Look at this. Chelsea on the swim team. That was a great exercise in humiliation.

ETHEL

Oh, stop it. You were a good diver.

CHELSEA

I wasn't a good diver. I was a good sport. I could never do a damn back flip.

ETHEL

Well, we were proud of you for trying.

CHELSEA

Right. Everyone got a big splash out of me trying.
Why do you think I subjected myself to all that? I
wasn't aiming for the 1956 Olympics, you know. I was
just trying to please Norman. Because he'd been a
diver, in the eighteen hundreds.

ETHEL

Can't you be home for five minutes without getting
started on the past?

CHELSEA

This house seems to set me off.

ETHEL

Well, it shouldn't. It's a nice house.

CHELSEA

I act like a big person everywhere else. I do. I'm in
charge in Los Angeles. I guess I've never grown up on
Golden Pond. Do you understand?

ETHEL

I don't think so.

CHELSEA

It doesn't matter. There's just something about coming back here that makes me feel like a little fat girl.

ETHEL

Sit down and tell me about your trip.

CHELSEA
(*An outburst*)
I don't want to sit down. Where were you all that
time? You never bailed me out.

ETHEL
I didn't know you needed bailing out.

CHELSEA
Well, I did.

ETHEL
Here we go again. You had a miserable childhood.
Your father was overbearing, your mother ignored
you. What else is new? Don't you think everyone looks
back on their childhood with some bitterness or regret about something? You are a big girl now, aren't
you tired of it all? You have this unpleasant chip on
your shoulder which is very unattractive. You only
come home when I beg you to, and when you get here
all you can do is be disagreeable about the past. Life
marches by, Chelsea, I suggest you get on with it.
(ETHEL *stands and glares at* CHELSEA)
You're such a nice person. Can't you think of something nice to say?

CHELSEA
I married Bill in Brussels.

ETHEL
You did what in Brussels?

CHELSEA

I married Bill.

ETHEL

Does it count in this country?

CHELSEA

'Fraid so.

ETHEL
(Stepping to CHELSEA *and kissing her)*
Well, bless you. Congratulations.

CHELSEA

Thank you.

ETHEL

You have an odd way of building up to good news.

CHELSEA

I know.

ETHEL

Bill seems very nice.

CHELSEA

He's better than nice. He's an adult, too. I decided to
go for an adult marriage this time. It's a standard
five-year contract with renewable options. If it doesn't
work out I still get to keep my gold caps.

ETHEL

What about Billy?

CHELSEA

Bill gets to keep Billy.

ETHEL

Will Billy live with you?

CHELSEA

Yes. That's part of the reason Bill had to get back to LA. He's murdering his ex-wife. She doesn't want the kid anyway.

ETHEL

Do you?

CHELSEA

Yes.

ETHEL

Well, I'm so pleased.

CHELSEA

Nothing to it. I'm twice as old as you were when you married Norman. Think that means anything?

ETHEL

I hope it means that Bill will be only half as much trouble. Norman will be so surprised.

CHELSEA

I'll bet.

ETHEL

All he wants is for you to be happy.

CHELSEA

Could have fooled me. He always makes me feel like I've got my shoes on the wrong feet.

ETHEL

That's just his manner. He enjoys keeping people on their toes.

CHELSEA

I'm glad *he* gets pleasure out of it.

ETHEL

Dear God, how long do you plan to keep this up? Hmm?

CHELSEA

I don't know. I . . . can't talk to him. I've never been able to.

ETHEL

Have you ever *tried*?

CHELSEA

Yes, we've discussed the relative stupidity of Puerto Rican baseball players. I don't even know him.

ETHEL

Well, he'll be along any minute. I'll be happy to introduce you. You don't get to know a person by staying away for years at a time.

CHELSEA

I know. Maybe someday we can try to be friends.

ETHEL

Chelsea, Norman is eighty years old. He has heart palpitations and a problem remembering things. When exactly do you expect this friendship to begin?

CHELSEA

I don't know. . . . I'm afraid of him.

ETHEL

Well, he's afraid of you. You should get along fine.
(NORMAN *arrives on the porch, resembling a wet rooster. As he enters,* ETHEL *rushes to him.* CHELSEA *stands back*)
Norman Thayer, you're soaking wet.

NORMAN

Yes, I know. It's raining. The damn loons are having a good laugh.
(*He sees* CHELSEA)
Well, well, well. Look at you.

CHELSEA

Hello.

NORMAN

I thought you weren't coming till the fifteenth.

CHELSEA

Today's the fifteenth.

NORMAN

Huh?

ETHEL

'Fraid so. What have you done with Billy?

NORMAN

Billy? He's swimming home.
(BILLY *arrives on the porch, laden down with the
gear. He, too, is drenched.* ETHEL *opens the door
and he steps in*)

BILLY

Guess what? It's raining.

ETHEL

Oh, for Lord's sake. Norman, help him with this stuff.

NORMAN

Tsk.
(*He walks over and transfers a few items from*
BILLY *to the floor*)

ETHEL

You two need constant supervision, I declare.
(BILLY *spots* CHELSEA)

BILLY

Hey! Look at you.

CHELSEA

Hey, kid.
(*She steps to him and hugs him*)

BILLY

How ya doin'?

CHELSEA

Not too shabby.

BILLY

What are you doing here?

CHELSEA

I was in the neighborhood, I thought I'd stop by.

BILLY

All right! Where's the dentist?

CHELSEA

He went ahead. He's going to call you tonight.

ETHEL
(*Taking* BILLY *by the collar*)

Would you please march upstairs and deposit yourself in a warm shower? Come on. You can talk to the
nice lady later. She has news for you which you can't
hear till you're dry.
(*She prods him up the stairs*)

NORMAN

What news?

BILLY
(*Turning back*)

Chelsea, you should have seen the bass I caught this
morning.
(*He holds his hands wide apart*)

NORMAN

Ha!

BILLY

Five pounds easy.

NORMAN

Ha!

BILLY

But then I saw this depressed look on Norman's face so I decided to let it go.

NORMAN and BILLY

Ha! Ha! Ha!
(BILLY *exits*)

ETHEL

Are you two going to be all right alone? I'm sure you can find something to talk about.

NORMAN

Yes. We can talk about the fact that the little person gets to take a shower while I develop pneumonia.

ETHEL

You're a tough old buzzard. Aren't you?
(*She exits.* NORMAN *scowls after her, then he turns to* CHELSEA)

NORMAN

Tough old buzzard. Don't these little endearments make your heart go pit-a-pat?

CHELSEA

Yes.
(*They study each other a moment*)

NORMAN

Did you hear what the stupid Yankees did?

CHELSEA

No.
(*Carefully*)
I don't want to talk about baseball.

NORMAN

Oh. I was just going to mention something you might
have found interesting, but it doesn't matter.

CHELSEA

I want to talk about us.

NORMAN

What about us?

CHELSEA

You want to sit down?

NORMAN
(*Nervous*)
Should I? I've already started a puddle here; perhaps
I'd better stand.

CHELSEA
(*Smiling*)
I just wanted to say . . . that I'm sorry.

NORMAN

Fine. No problem.

CHELSEA

Don't you want to know what I'm sorry about?

NORMAN

I suppose so.

CHELSEA

Um. I'm sorry that our communication has been so bad. That my . . . that I've been walking around with a chip on my shoulder.

NORMAN

Oh.

CHELSEA

I'm sorry I didn't come to your retirement dinner.

NORMAN

Oh. That was some time ago, you know.

CHELSEA

Yes. I know.

NORMAN

Well, you really missed something there. I gave them quite a speech.

CHELSEA

I heard about it. I heard you were very funny.

NORMAN

I was. I was a scream.

CHELSEA

I'm sorry I missed it.

NORMAN

Well . . .

CHELSEA

Um, I think it would be a good idea if we tried . . . to have the kind of relationship we're supposed to have.

NORMAN

What kind of relationship are we supposed to have?

CHELSEA

Um. Like a father and a daughter.

NORMAN

Ah. Well. Just in the knick of time, huh?

CHELSEA

No.

NORMAN

Worried about the will, are you? I'm leaving everything to you, except what I'm taking with me.

CHELSEA

Stop it.
(She steps to him)
I don't want anything. We've been mad at each other for too long.

NORMAN

Oh. I didn't realize we were mad. I thought we just didn't like each other.

CHELSEA

I want to be your friend.

NORMAN

Oh. Okay. Does this mean you're going to come around more often. I may not last eight more years, you know.

CHELSEA

Tsk. I'll come around more often.

NORMAN

Well. It would mean a lot to your mother.

CHELSEA

Okay.
  (*They look at each other a moment, nothing more to say*)
Now you want to tell me about the Yankees?

NORMAN

The Yankees? They're bums. Your mother said you had some news, what is it?

CHELSEA
  (*Smiling*)
I got married in Brussels.

NORMAN

You did? In Brussels. Isn't that nice?

CHELSEA

It is. It's the best thing that's ever happened to me. He makes me very happy.

NORMAN

That's good. He speak English?

CHELSEA

Tsk. I married Bill.

NORMAN

Oh, Bill. That *is* nice.

ETHEL
(*Offstage*)

Next!

NORMAN

What is she screaming about?

CHELSEA

You're next in the shower.

NORMAN

Oh.
> (*He turns to go. Turns back to* CHELSEA)

Talk to you later.
> (CHELSEA *smiles.* ETHEL *appears on the landing and calls down*)

ETHEL

Next!

NORMAN

Good God. This place is starting to sound like a brothel.

(*He climbs the stairs, meeting* ETHEL *midway*)

ETHEL

What do you know about brothels?

NORMAN

I know a lot about brothels. Brothels is where Chelthea married her thweetheart. Ha ha ha.

ETHEL

Isn't it wonderful?

NORMAN

Yeth.

(*To* CHELSEA)

Yes.

(*To* ETHEL)

Here now, see if you can get us a discount on the dental work.

(*He exits.* ETHEL *steps down into the room. She looks at* CHELSEA, *who shrugs. There is the sound of a motorboat*)

ETHEL

Oh, my goodness, Now here's Charlie. This *is* like a brothel.

(*She opens the door*)

CHELSEA

Charlie! Maybe he'd like to take a shower, too.

ETHEL

Come on up, dear, and have some coffee. Oh, my goodness, the coffee! I'd better get some biscuits. Charlie gets dangerous if you don't feed him.

(She exits into the kitchen. CHARLIE *parades across the porch in his bright slicker. He calls through the door)*

CHARLIE

Morning.

(He sees CHELSEA *and opens the door)*

Well, Holy Mackinoly.

CHELSEA

Hello. What's new?

CHARLIE
(Laughing)

It's raining.

CHELSEA

So I've been told.

*(*CHARLIE *takes off his jacket and hat)*

Look at you. Fat as an old cat.

CHARLIE

Look at you.

CHELSEA

Not quite as fat.

CHARLIE

Chelsea Mackinelsea.

CHELSEA

Charlie Mackinarlie.

CHARLIE

When did you get back?

CHELSEA

This morning.

CHARLIE

Bring the boyfriend?

CHELSEA

No. He's not my boyfriend anymore.

CHARLIE

Oh, no?

CHELSEA

No, I married him.

CHARLIE

What the heck for?

CHELSEA

I felt sorry for him.
     (ETHEL *enters with the coffee and a plate of bis-*
     cuits)

ETHEL

You're early this morning, Charlie. What happened?

CHARLIE

I'm doing the route backwards.

ETHEL

You are?

CHARLIE

Yuh. Thought I'd like to see what it was like. I've been having these little dizzy spells lately, and I thought maybe it was due to going around the lake in the same direction for thirty years.

ETHEL

Are you going to be going backward for the next thirty years, do you think?

CHARLIE

I might.

ETHEL

You'll be just like the rest of the world then. Sit down if you're dizzy. I don't want you falling all over the room.

(*The three of them sit.* CHARLIE *stares at* CHELSEA)

CHARLIE
(*To* ETHEL)

Chelsea Mackinelsea tells me she got herself married again.

ETHEL

Yes. Isn't it wonderful?

CHARLIE

I guess. That sort of puts me out of the running again, huh?

(*He laughs*)

The old maid mailman.

ETHEL

Oh, pooh. You could have anyone you wanted.

CHARLIE

That's not true, Ethel.

CHELSEA

You wouldn't have wanted me, Charlie. We're too good of friends to be married.

CHARLIE

I guess. Holy Mackinoly. That kid Billy gonna be your son now?

CHELSEA

Yes.

CHARLIE

Huh.

(*He laughs*)

Well. Congratulations.

CHELSEA

Thank you.

CHARLIE

How long do you expect to be around this trip?

CHELSEA

Another week.

ETHEL

Good!

CHARLIE

Why don't you come ride the mailboat one time? I'll
let you drive it.

CHELSEA

Okay.

CHARLIE

You know, it's funny. I was thinking of you just this
morning. I was coming down Koochakiyi Shores, and
I almost pulled into the little cove where the big dock
used to be. There's three cottages in there now. One is
the Bensons, I don't know the other two, I don't de-
liver in there. But this morning there was something
in my mind, and for a minute there I thought I was a
kid again.

(*He laughs*)

ETHEL

There's a lot of that going around, Charlie.

CHARLIE

Yuh? That happen to you, too?
(*To* CHELSEA)
I can remember so clearly coming in there on my
uncle's boat. *The Mariah*, remember?
(CHELSEA *smiles and nods*)

I'd get up on the deck with that big mail bag for the whole camp, and all those crazy girls would come running down, and I used to feel so important. I'd swing the bag out onto the dock, and then I'd pick up the outgoing mail, and somewhere in there, I'd look for you. And you'd always be standing in the back, kind of all alone. And you'd smile at me, and I'd feel like I was the best thing going.

CHELSEA
You were.

CHARLIE
Yuh, I guess I was. Those were the times.

CHELSEA
I remember, in the evenings, sometimes, you'd come along by Koochakiyi Shores, with your brother Tom, and anchor your boat and pretend to fish.

CHARLIE
Yuh. We never caught a single one either. We rarely even brought bait. We just liked to hear all you girls sing, and I'd hope to see you. It would start to get dark, and you'd have a campfire, and sing those stupid songs.

ETHEL
(*Singing*)
I can hear the echo
Of my song,
From my tent on the bank

CHARLIE
(*Overlapping*)

That's one of 'em.

ETHEL
(*Continues singing*)

Of the lake
Called Golden Pond.
On Golden Pond.

CHARLIE
(*He laughs*)

It was such a sad song. Used to give me the creeps.
Yuh, yuh, yuh.

> (*He laughs.* CHELSEA *stands and grabs* ETHEL's
> *hand, pulls her up. They stand in front of* CHAR-
> LIE. CHELSEA *begins the song and the dance, and
> then* ETHEL *joins in*)

CHELSEA

We are the girls from Camp Koochakiyi.
You can tell who we are . . .
By the gleam in our eyes.

(*They laugh*)

CHELSEA and ETHEL

Our minds are clear and our hearts
Are strong.
We are dancing here, but we won't be long.
There will soon be deer where there now
Are fawns.
But we'll remember our years on Golden Pond.
On Golden Pond.

(CHARLIE *claps*)

SCENE TWO

The middle of September. Late morning.

The room is cluttered again. The tables are back in from the porch, the dust covers are back in place, the dining chairs piled upside down on the oak table. Outside, the sky is bright and blue.

After a moment, ETHEL *enters from the kitchen, carrying a cardboard box. She sets it down on a table, and goes back into the kitchen. She wears a tidy pantsuit now.*

NORMAN *comes in the down left door. He is dressed in his "traveling clothes," neat slacks and a jacket. He sees the box and picks it up. He holds it, looking about the room. He wanders up to the platform, and sets the box down. He examines his fishing gear quickly, and then walks up the stairs and into the hallway above.*

ETHEL *comes back into the room with another box. She begins to set it down, realizes the first is gone, looks for it. She sees it on the platform and stares at it, puzzled. She sets down the second box and then*

169

goes up the steps for the first, which she carries
back down, and then out the downstage door.

NORMAN *comes down the stairs, carrying a fishing*
pole. He leans it against the couch. He picks up
the box ETHEL *left and begins to carry it to the*
door, thinks of something, and crosses back to the
platform, and sets it down. He goes to the hat rack
and studies the collection. ETHEL *comes in, looks*
for the box, sees it on the platform.

ETHEL

Norman, what in the world are you doing with the boxes?

NORMAN

Nothing. Which one of these hats is your favorite?

ETHEL

You moved this box and you moved the other box, too. Are we moving out or in?

NORMAN

Oh. This box. I'm carrying this box to the car. I'm helping you.

ETHEL

You certainly have a roundabout way of doing it. The car is in the back, you know.

NORMAN

I know. Which hat is your favorite?

ETHEL

I dislike them all equally.
(*She carries the box downstage*)

NORMAN

I was going to take that box.

ETHEL

Yes. It's where you were going to take it that had me
concerned, so I'm taking it myself.
          (*Stopping by the fireplace*)
What is your old fish pole doing here?

NORMAN

I fixed it. I fixed the reel, and I retied the splints.

ETHEL

What's it doing here?

NORMAN

It's waiting to go to the car. I'm going to mail it to
Billy.

ETHEL

What? You can't mail a fish pole.

NORMAN

Of course I can. I'm a taxpayer. He may want to go
fishing. I assume they have fish in California.

ETHEL

Well . . .
          (*She looks up.* NORMAN *is now wearing one of the
          floppy hats*)
What are you doing with that terrible hat?

NORMAN
(*Crossing down*)
I'm mailing it to Billy with the fish pole. You can't fish
without a hat.

ETHEL
He tries fishing with that thing on his head anywhere
outside of Golden Pond, he'll probably be arrested.

NORMAN
Not in California he won't.

ETHEL
Well, bring it then. There's barely room.
(NORMAN *opens the door.* ETHEL *steps out, but he
lingers. He wanders across to the bookshelves and
studies them. He pulls down a book. The phone
rings.* NORMAN *looks up, startled.* ETHEL *comes
back in*)
Did you get lost?

NORMAN
No, I'm over here.
(*The phone rings again*)
The phone's ringing.

ETHEL
Well, what do you know? I suppose we'd better answer it.

NORMAN
Yes.
(*She steps to the phone and picks it up*)

ETHEL

Hello? . . . Hello? . . . Oh, hello . . . I'm fine, thank
you. How are you? . . . Good. . . . We're leaving
right now . . . thank you . . .

NORMAN

Who is it?

ETHEL
(*Covering the receiver*)

I have no idea.
(*Into the phone*)
Who is this? . . . Oh, Bill! How are you? . . . Good.
(*To* NORMAN)
It's Bill.

NORMAN

Bill? Oh. Bill!

ETHEL

Thank you, Bill. . . . Well, we'd love to. . . . Yes.
. . . Of course, put her on. I know this is costing you
a fortune.

NORMAN

I'm surprised he didn't reverse the charges. Chelsea's
first husband always used to.
(*He sits in his covered chair and begins to read*)

ETHEL

Hi, darling. . . . Yes. We're just leaving. Two more
boxes and say goodbye to the lake, and that will be

that. . . . Oh, no. Everyone else is gone practically.
. . . Your house sounds wonderful. Send us some
pictures. We would love to, dear. Maybe in January.
. . . Instead of Florida, yes. We'll discuss it. . . . If I
can get Norman to accept the fact that Los Angeles is
part of the United States, it shouldn't be too much
trouble. He's still convinced you need a passport to
get out there, and yellow-fever shots and everything.
. . . Well, bless you. . . . Of course. I'll get him.
Norman, she wants to talk to you.

NORMAN
(*Looking up from his book*)
Tsk. I've just started my book.

ETHEL
Norman, she wants to talk to you.

NORMAN
Why would she want to talk to me?

ETHEL
Get it in gear, Norman.
(*He stands.* ETHEL *speaks into the phone*)
He's coming, dear. Give my love to Billy. We hope to
see you soon. Yes. Bye.
(NORMAN *flings his book onto the couch and*
ETHEL *hands him the phone*)

NORMAN
What will I say to her?

ETHEL
You'll think of something.

NORMAN
(*Into the phone*)

Hello. . . . Um. How's the weather? . . . Oh. No earthquakes?

(ETHEL *shakes her head. She picks up the fishing pole, and takes the hat off* NORMAN's *head. She carries them both outside*)

. . . Good. . . . Oh, I don't know if we'll be able to come way out there. Ethel's health isn't what it could be, you know. . . . No, nothing serious. She's just more ornery than usual. . . . Oh, no, I'm in great form myself. Just a lot of pain. Nothing to worry about. . . . Well, we'll certainly consider it. . . . Oh, thank you. . . . Oh, well. I love you, too.

(*He's embarrassed*)

Yes.

(*Brightly*)

Billy there? . . . Good. Could I speak to him? . . . Yes, we will. You have fun, too—the three of you. . . . Okay, Chelsea. Bye!

(*He stares off while waiting for* BILLY)

. . . Hello, cool breeze. How's the chicks? . . . No, the fish are all gone, somewhere. . . . I don't know. They go to sleep, I believe. . . . No, I don't think it would be right for me to wake them. . . . How's your reading? . . . Don't tell me! How wonderful. . . . Yes, I know, but it's pronounced Doo-ma . . . Say that . . . *Doo-ma* . . . Tres bien. . . . That's okay, run along. I expect you'll want to do a little cruising on your way to school. I'll tell her. . . . Yes, Billy. . . . Well, I miss you, too. . . . Listen, Ethel and I are coming out to visit, you know. . . . Oh, yes. In the winter. . . . I'm *not* bullshitting you. . . . Yes. Me, too. Bye! Adieu, mon vieux.

(*He hangs up, feeling quite chipper.* ETHEL *enters*)

I talked to Billy.

ETHEL

How nice.

NORMAN

He said he wants you to mail him some tollhouse cookies.

ETHEL

Oh, he does, does he?

NORMAN

Yes. Says Chelsea makes them but they're not as good.

ETHEL

Huh. Well, that's the way it is with us grandmothers, you know. Chelsea mention us going out there for a visit?

NORMAN

I think she did.

ETHEL

I guess we could, don't you think?

NORMAN

Well . . . I guess so.

ETHEL

I think they're going to make a go of it.

NORMAN

What do you mean?

ETHEL

The marriage. I think it's a success.

NORMAN

It's lasted over a month already.

ETHEL

It makes me feel so good to think that Chelsea is finally settling down.

NORMAN

Yes. Want to play a quick game of Parcheesi before we go? Loser drives.

ETHEL

No. Haven't you been humiliated enough? You owe me four million dollars.

NORMAN

Double or nothing?

ETHEL

When we get home, Norman. We've got the whole winter ahead of us.

NORMAN

Yes.

ETHEL

Come on, let's get the other boxes, and be gone.
(*She heads into the kitchen.* NORMAN *stays where
he is, looking about.* ETHEL *calls from offstage*)
Norman! Would you come here?
(*He crosses to the kitchen door*)

NORMAN

What is it?
(*He exits*)

ETHEL
(*Offstage*)
Get the last box if it's not too heavy.
(*She enters*)

NORMAN
(*Offstage*)
Of course it's not too heavy. Good God, this is heavy!

ETHEL

Tsk. Well, wait and I'll help you with it then.

NORMAN
(*Offstage*)
You're trying to kill me.

ETHEL

I've thought about it.
(*She carries her box downstage as he comes out
with his*)

NORMAN

Good God!
(*He crosses to the platform. She waits for him at the door. He moves slowly*)
Whatever have you got in here?

ETHEL

My mother's china. I've decided to take it to Wilmington and use it there.
(NORMAN *is feeling his way down the steps*)
We hardly ever eat off it here. Are you all right?

NORMAN

Yes. Your mother never liked me.

ETHEL

Oh, stop. She loved you.

* NORMAN

Then why did she have such heavy china? Oh, my God.

ETHEL

Set it down if it's too much trouble. Norman!
(*He is in pain. He leans against the couch, still holding the box*)
Norman! Put the box down!

NORMAN
(*He groans*)
Unh. I don't want to break your mother's china. Ouch.

ETHEL

Norman!

> (*She drops her box with a tremendous crash. She runs to* NORMAN. *He drops his box*)

NORMAN

Whoops.

> (*He sags against the couch, clutching his chest. She tries to hold him*)

ETHEL

Sit down, you fool.

> (*She helps him to the couch. He slumps*)

Where's your medicine?

NORMAN

I don't know. You packed.

ETHEL

Oh, God! What did I do with it? I'm afraid it's in the car.

> (*She runs to the door and exits, her speech continuing outside*)

Which suitcase? *Which suitcase?*

> (NORMAN *grimaces, clutches his chest. He glances around the room, spots the book on the couch beside him. He reaches for it, opens it, grimaces again.*
> ETHEL *runs back in with a little jar*)

What are you doing, you nitwit? Give me that book!

> (*She grabs it and throws it onto the floor*)

NORMAN

What are you doing?

ETHEL

I'm trying to save your life, damn you. Whoever de-
signed these caps is a madman. There, take this and
put it under your tongue.
          (*She holds out a pill*)

NORMAN

What is it?

ETHEL

Nitroglycerin. Put it under your tongue.

NORMAN

You must be mad. I'll blow up.

ETHEL

Do it!
          (NORMAN *takes the pill. She kneels beside him,*
          watching. He breathes deeply and leans his head
          back, his eyes closed. ETHEL *begins to weep*)
Oh, dear God, don't take him now. You don't want
him, he's a poop. Norman? Norman!

NORMAN
          (*His eyes closed*)
Maybe you should call a doctor. We can afford it.

ETHEL

Oh, yes!
          (*She jumps up*)

Of course. I should have done that. Dear God.
> (*She rushes to the phone and dials "0"*)

Hello, hello. Dear God. How are you feeling, Norman?

NORMAN

Oh, pretty good. How are you?

ETHEL

Norman, how's the angina?

NORMAN

The what?

ETHEL

The pain, dammit!

NORMAN

Oh. It's pretty good, as pain goes.

ETHEL

Is the medicine doing anything?

NORMAN

No.

ETHEL

Why don't they answer the phone?

NORMAN

Who'd you call?

ETHEL

The stupid operator.
> (*Into the receiver*)

Hello? . . . Hello?
> (*Getting frantic*)

Hello, hello, hello, hello, hello, hello! Whatever is the matter with her?

NORMAN

She's slow.

ETHEL

How do you feel now?

NORMAN

I don't know.

ETHEL

Are you planning to die? Is that what you're up to? Well, while I'm waiting for this moron to answer the phone, let me just say something to you, Norman Thayer, Junior. I would rather you didn't.

NORMAN

Really?

ETHEL

Yes! This stupid, stupid, woman. I'm going to have to call a hospital directly.
> (*She slams down the phone, and pulls out the phone book*)

Where do you look for hospitals? Yellow pages. Hospital, hospital. They're not listed. Oh, wait. . . .

NORMAN

Ethel.

ETHEL
(*Fearing the worst*)

Yes! What is it!?

NORMAN

Come here.

ETHEL

Oh, God.
(*She rushes over and kneels by his side*)
Yes, Norman. My darling.

NORMAN

Ethel.

ETHEL
(*Crying*)

Yes. I'm here. Oh, Norman.

NORMAN

Ethel.

ETHEL

Yes, yes, yes.

NORMAN

Ethel.

ETHEL

What is it?

NORMAN

Ethel. I think I feel all right now.

ETHEL

Are you serious?

NORMAN

I think so. My heart's stopped hurting. Maybe I'm dead.

ETHEL

It really doesn't hurt?

NORMAN

Really doesn't. Shall I dance to prove it?

ETHEL
(*Falling against him*)
Oh, Norman. Oh, thank God. I love you so much.
(*A moment passes. She cries.* NORMAN *puts his arm around her*)

NORMAN

Now my heart's starting to hurt again.
(*He holds her close*)
Sorry about your mother's china.
(*He pulls himself forward to look at it*)

ETHEL

You're such a poop. Sit still and don't move.

NORMAN

Are you mad at me?

ETHEL

Yes. Why did you strain yourself? You know better.

NORMAN

I was showing off. Trying to turn you on.

ETHEL

Well, you succeeded. There's no need for you to try
that sort of thing again.

NORMAN

Good.
> (For a long moment they sit without moving. She
> stares at him as though she's trying to memorize
> him. He smiles down at her. The moment passes
> and she glances away)

ETHEL

This is my favorite time of year on Golden Pond. No
bugs.

NORMAN

Nope.

ETHEL

Except for that spider up there.

NORMAN
> (Looking up)

Good God. He's a biggie.

ETHEL

Yes. Well, I'd like to do him in, but I'm afraid I don't
have the energy.

NORMAN

Get him first thing next year.

ETHEL

Right.

(*A pause*)

Norman.

(*A pause*)

This was the first time I've really felt we're going to die.

NORMAN

I've known it all along.

ETHEL

Yes, I know. But when I looked at you across the room, I could really see you dead. I could see you in your blue suit and a white starched shirt, lying in Thomas's Funeral Parlor on Bradshaw Street, your hands folded on your stomach, a little smile on your face.

NORMAN

How did I look?

ETHEL

Not good, Norman.

NORMAN

Which tie was I wearing?

ETHEL

I don't know.

NORMAN

How about the one with the picture of the man fishing? Did you pack that one?

ETHEL

Shut up, Norman.
(*Pause*)
You've been talking about dying ever since I met you. It's been your favorite topic of conversation. And I've *had* to think about it. Our parents, my sister and brother, your brother, their wives, our dearest friends, practically everyone from the old days on Golden Pond, all dead. I've seen death, and touched death, and feared it. But today was the first time I've felt it.

NORMAN

How's it feel?

ETHEL

It feels . . . odd. Cold, I guess. But not that bad, really. Almost comforting, not so frightening, not such a bad place to go. I don't know.

NORMAN
(*He holds her head for a moment*)
Want to see if you can find my book?

ETHEL

Here it is.
(*She picks it up from the floor*)
Going to take it?

NORMAN

Nope. It belongs here. Put it on the shelf.
(*She crosses and returns the book to its place*)
I'll read it next year.

ETHEL

Yes. Next year.
(*She wanders around behind the couch*)
We'll have the whole summer to read and pick berries
and play Monopoly, and Billy can come for as long as
he likes, and you two can fish, and I'll make cookies,
and life will go on, won't it?

NORMAN

I hope so.

ETHEL

I guess I'll go down and say goodbye to the lake. Feel
like coming?

NORMAN

Yes

(*He rises slowly*)

ETHEL

You sure you're strong enough?

NORMAN

I think so. If I fall over face first in the water you'll
know I wasn't.

ETHEL
(*Waiting for him*)
Well, go easy, for God's sake. I'm only good for one
near miss a day.

NORMAN
(Getting up to her slowly)
Hello there.

ETHEL
Hi.

NORMAN
(Taking her in his arms)
Want to dance? Or would you rather just suck face?

ETHEL
You really are a case, you know.
(Call of a loon)

NORMAN
Yes.

ETHEL
My word, Norman, the loons. They've come round to
say goodbye.

NORMAN
How nice.

ETHEL
Just the two of them now. Little baby's grown up and
moved to Los Angeles or somewhere.

NORMAN
Yes.
(They kiss. A long gentle moment passes. They look
at one another, and then look away)

ETHEL

Well, let's go down.
   (*They exit. He follows her across the porch and
   down the steps*)
Hello, Golden Pond. We've come to say goodbye.

CURTAIN

About The Author

ERNEST THOMPSON was born November 6, 1949, in Bellows Falls, Vermont. He graduated with honors from American University, and has worked extensively as an actor. ON GOLDEN POND, his first produced play, enjoyed a long run on Broadway (where it was voted Best Play of the 1978–79 Season by the Broadway Drama Guild) and has been performed in hundreds of productions throughout the world. Thompson's other writing includes the plays THE WEST SIDE WALTZ, A SENSE OF HUMOR, THE KINDNESS OF STRANGERS, LESSONS, and ANSWERS; and the film ON GOLDEN POND.

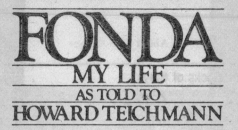

MENTOR Bo...

**Edited by Slyvan Barnet,
Morton Berman, and William Burto**

☐ **EIGHT GREAT TRAGEDIES.** The great dramatic literature of the ages. Eight memorable tragedies by Aeschylus, Euripides, Sophocles, Shakespeare, Ibsen, Strindberg, Yeats, and O'Neill. With essays on tragedy by Aristotle, Emerson and others. (#ME1911—$2.50)

☐ **EIGHT GREAT COMEDIES.** Complete texts of eight masterpieces of comic drama by Aristophanes, Machiavelli, Shakespeare, Molière, John Gay, Wilde, Chekhov, and Shaw. Includes essays on comedy by four distinguished critics and scholars. (#ME2008—$2.95)

☐ **THE GENIUS OF THE EARLY ENGLISH THEATRE.** Complete plays including three anonymous plays—"Abraham and Isaac," "The Second Shepherd's Play," and "Everyman," and Marlowe's "Doctor Faustus," Shakespeare's "Macbeth," Jonson's "Volpone," and Milton's "Samson Agonistes," with critical essays.
(#ME1889—$2.50)